OLD AND COLD

OLD AND COLD

– Jim Nisbet –

THE OVERLOOK PRESS
NEW YORK, NY

This edition first published in paperback in the United States in 2012 by

The Overlook Press, Peter Mayer Publishers, Inc.
141 Wooster Street
New York, NY 10012
www.overlookpress.com
For bulk and special sales, please contact sales@overlookny.com

The passage on page 52 is cited from *The Unabomber Manifesto: Industrial Society and Its Future* © 2005 by Theodore Kaczynski. The poem on page 74 is "The World Is Too Much With Us" by William Wordsworth.

Cataloging-in-Publication Data is available from the Library of Congress

Book design and typeformatting by Bernard Schleifer
Manufactured in the United States of America
FIRST EDITION
2 4 6 8 10 9 7 5 3 1
ISBN 978-1-59020-915-8

For
Jean-Pierre Deloux
frère, compère, corsaire

You can do whatever you want,
whatever you hear.

—JOANNE BRACKEEN

Death nudged him as he lay there. There was an old
Latin saying about the darkness. *Spatien pro morte facite.*
Make room for death.

—HOWARD FAST, *Spartacus*

ONE

HERE WE GO AGAIN. IF THE SHIT CONTINUES LIKE THIS, I'M going to anneal the ferromagnesian nest under the bridge and take up smoking. It should be near an internet cafe so I'll have access to streaming pornography. There's deprivation, and there's deprivation.

I don't know how it came to this. Yes, I do. There could have been no other path. It's the way I led my life. Pillar to post, paycheck to paycheck, and, finally, inadequate Social Security dribble to inadequate Social Security dribble. I took it early, too. The theory was, is, you never know, you could die tomorrow, and then where'll that larger dribble be, the one you could take if you waited till you were sixty-six, or seventy? Do the math, the smart money said. Besides, the smart money added, with a knuckle chuck to the shoulder with the pin in it, you cut drool with a little dribble? It makes a larger stain on your bib.

Yo. You start taking your Social Security when you're immediately able? At, say, in my case, sixty-two? At, say, in my case, seven hundred and sixty-three spermatazoa a month, with which you are to fertilize the eggs of commerce? After four years, which is the difference between sixty-two and sixty-six, pay attention, that comes to

$$4 \text{ years x } 12 \text{ months/year} = 48 \text{ months}$$
$$48 \text{ months x } \$763/\text{month} = \$36,624$$

In other words, $9156 per year

Now, if you're like me, and you're living under a bridge, or on a weed-bearded Chris-Craft listing at anchor lo these fifteen years in some stinking gunkhole, as close as possible to some fast-food joint so you can walk to it, to where they have one-dollar blue-plate Depression Lunch Specials, you need to be thinking about this shit. Because some people will tell you, no, no, man, keep working. To whom you might say, hey, fecalface, have you ever levered fishheads and contaminated ice with a grain scoop up and out the hold of a purse seiner at eleven dollars an hour when you're 62 years old? Just keep your head down, they will tell you. Keep working. Hold out. You'll make more money, period. Cause, you know, like

$11/hour x 40 hours/week x 50 weeks/year[1] = $22,000 per year!

I had no idea, you say. Pass the non-steroidal anti-inflamma-tory medication. That's why I get the big money, the smart money says, ten percent of every dribble, to figure this shit out for you. So now, bear with me. If you wait until you can take your full retirement, at age 66, they'll give you $1063 per month. That's a three-hundred-dollar difference. It's also a four year difference, you point out. You know what an old man like you can do, the smart money says, ignoring you, with an extra three hundred dollars a month? That should just about cover the cost of non-steroidal anti-inflammatory medication, you suggest. Not funny, says the big money, not funny at all. I was in proximity to a fancy cafe just this morning, you say, looking to retrieve a copy of today's paper off an abandoned table, and I nostalgically noticed that a Bombay Sapphire martini cost seventeen dollars in that joint. You got that three hundred bucks, the smart money points

---

[1] Figuring two weeks/year vacation South of Market.

out, you can drink 17.65 martinis a month. You roll your eyes like
they're a pair of half-olives in an open-face sandwich. Careful,
I'm hungry. How many Martinis does a sixty-six year-old man
need? Somewhere between two and five a night, you answer
without hesitation, depending on the condition my condition is
in. My lower-case g god, the smart money says, that's a minimum
of fifty-six in a leap-year February to a maximum hundred and
fifty-five martinis in a thirty-one day month. You smack your lips:
hell, you say, it takes the better part of the first one just to wash
down the non-steroidal etc., not to mention the spookily sentient
open face sandwich. Put another way, the smart money persists,
that's $952 for a relatively temperate leap-year February, ranging
to something like $2635 for a balls-out binge any of the seven
thirty-one-day months out of the year. That's depressing. Which
provokes a thought. Yes? How much money would it cost to keep
on hand enough ibuprofen sufficient to feed the cuerpo 800 mil-
ligrams a night? I think they're about five bucks apiece, the smart
money says, the eight hundreds. The smart money shrugs.
Generic, you get them a little cheaper. So that's…A hundred and
fifty bucks a month, the smart money interpolates. And where is
that money supposed to come from, you ask. Out of your twenty-two kay a year, the smart money replies, restating the obvious.
Hey, you say, what's a progressive writer do? I don't know, the
smart money mutters tiredly, what? She spends all day restating
the obvious and all night dreaming about it, you reply gleefully, I
love that definition. The smart money makes a little puckered up
face like maybe he just caught a whiff of formaldehyde drifting
over the ditch. I'm a fiscal conservative, the smart money says.
But you know what? you say. What, the smart money says. In
order for the payments to kick in at the higher rate when you're
sixty-six to achieve parity with the lower payments you, of all
people, should have started taking when you were sixty-two—

I didn't know what time it was, you interject—fourteen point seven years have to elapse. The smart money looks startled. Say what? Let's do some simple algebra, you suggest. You? the smart money responds. Algebra? Sure, you reply.

$$66 \text{ years} - 62 \text{ years} = 4 \text{ years}$$
$$4 \text{ years} \times 12 \text{ months/year} = 48 \text{ months}$$

I see you're keeping your units straight, observes the smart money. You keep your units straight, you say, you keep yourself straight. Easy does it, the smart money forewarns, or I'll smack you with the calculus. One day at a time, you reply. That'll be the day, the smart money says. So, you continue, how much was that payment at 62? Seven sixty-three, the smart money replies.

$$48 \text{ months} \times \$763/\text{month} = \$36,624$$

Okay? Watch me now. I'm watching. So, after forty-eight months at seven sixty-three a month you got thirty-six thousand, six hundred twenty-four dollars. What if your doppelgänger holds out, he continues to scoop fishheads and ice for another four years, until he can take full retirement. The question becomes, at what point have you and your doppelgänger drawn equal totals of Social Security checks? That's an interesting question, the smart money admits. Let's call that point in time the moment of parity, you stipulate to the smart money, and let's call gamma the number of months it takes to achieve the moment of parity. Fine by me, says the smart money. Okay, you say, now we need a field of grime. The entire face of this concrete abutment is one big carbon footprint, the smart money says. Okay, you say, lend me your rabbit's foot. Not on your life, says the smart money. Come on, man, you say, later this week we'll run it through the laundromat with the rest of your uniform. Unless you got some paper? No paper, laments the smart money. Fork it over. The smart money forks over the rabbit's foot. A single, tiny key is attached to it by a loop of beaded chain, the key to baggage left behind a long time ago. It's symbolic. And with its rabbit's foot, in the grime on the face of the bridge abutment, you inscribe some equations.

$$(48 \text{ months} \times \$763/\text{month}) + (\gamma \text{ months} \times \$763/\text{month})$$

$$= (\gamma \text{ months} \times \$1063/\text{month})$$

$$\$36{,}624 = (\gamma \text{ months} \times \$1063/\text{month}) - (\gamma \text{ months} \times \$763/\text{month})$$

$$\$36{,}624 = \gamma \times (\$1063 - \$763) = \gamma \times \$300$$

$$\gamma = \$36{,}624 / \$300 = 122.08 \text{ months}$$

$$122.08 \text{ months} / 12 \text{ months/year} = 10.17 \text{ years}$$

$$4 \text{ years} + 10.17 \text{ years} = 14.17 \text{ years @ parity}$$

See, you say, both of you, you and your doppelgänger, will be well into your decrepit seventies. Think fused disks and molybdenum parts. Damn, says the smart money. There's similar calculations you can do for the difference between sixty-two years and seventy years, and between sixty-six years and seventy years. Let me let me, says the smart money, wielding his rabbit's foot, and it's not long before the soot on the groin of the bridge abutment is crawling with figures. Hell's bells, says the smart money, it'll take fourteen point six eight years to achieve parity between the payments initiated at seventy as opposed to the lower ones initiated at sixty-six years of age. I just love algebra, you interject. And it will take, the smart money continues patiently, sixteen point seven five years to achieve parity between the sumtotal of higher payments initiated at seventy years of age as opposed to the lower payments initiated at sixty-two years of age. You'll be almost seventy-nine years old, the two of you point out, in unison. If you're still alive, again in unison. Say, the smart money adds, what if you take simple interest on these figures? How's that, you say. You know, you get seven sixty-three on month one and put it in the bank at so many percent compounded monthly. What are you to live on? We're not talking about living. Oh. So the next month, when the next seven sixty-three comes in, you add it to the first seven sixty-three, only now the first seven sixty-three is, say, seven seventy-two or something, so you have what they call over there in accounts receivable an aged total. I see what you're getting at, you say. You'll never catch up, the smart money says. It's kind of like an investment, you say. That's it, the smart money says. Highly theoretical, you point out. How's that? the smart money asks. Like all investments, you reply, it's highly theoretical. You mean, your personal investments, the smart money says. That's right, you say. All my life, all my investments have been highly theoretical. Take that Apple stock I should have bought, way back in 1985. Which gets us only a little anterior to taking up smoking and living under a bridge, the smart money says. That why you get the big money, you point out kindly, along with the occasional pubic louse. *Mallophaga* or *Anoplura*, the smart money asks without hesitation. I'm not sure, you admit readily, arresting the urge to scratch. You got a itch, the smart money says, you oughta scratch it. Is that what the smart money says? you say, scratching. They won't send that check to a post office box, the smart money reminds you. Another goddamn cost-of-living expense, you grouse, there oughta be a pleonasm. Is this circling back to the notion of progressive writing? the smart money asks. No, you reply, albeit with some uncertainty. Good, the smart money says, because I'm a fiscal conservative. What's that mean, anyway? you ask. In what context? the smart money hedges. What context? You wave a hand. *This* goddamn context. The smart money looks around. Pretty grim. A lot of gravel and Scotch broom. Gravel is ubiquitous, and Scotch broom will grow anywhere, you point out. It would appear to be so, says the smart money. No use taking up smoking, anyway. How's that, you say. No cigarettes, is the reply; besides, while orally they may be equivalent, numismatically they cost more than martinis. You're not being helpful, you say. Lay off them cigarettes, the smart money points out, maybe you'll achieve the parity before you achieve the lung cancer. Got to get a fixed address first, you reiterate, then start to get the checks, then worry about the lung cancer, you hear what I'm saying? Is this circling back around...To fiscal conservatism, you're exactly correct. That'll be the day, the smart money says. Say, you say, which side are you on, in this equation? The side that's going to come up with lunch. Why, just the other day, a man handed us his lunch. Just the other day? That was...We were looking more pitiable than usual. That was...Pitiable? You mean feedable. A pity-feed? ...several years ago, it seems to me. Another thing, without those social services, you couldn't tell if you had the lung cancer or not. Really? Doesn't it make it hard to breathe? I wouldn't know. You should take up smoking and find out. Why not take up social services? You know, cut to the chase. I spent my whole life chasing. You haven't stirred a finger. Not a dactyl. Forswear. I'm serious. Everything's serious. Compute. Seriously? Renounce. What's left? Decline. Done. Parity? Repertory. Ah, repertory. The repository. What's left? Not a gimmick. Nary a trick. Sub-par chicanery, below the bottom of the hole, underwater, submerged, under obscure glass. See the way that woman is looking at you? Me? She's looking at you. Stand up straight, she's wondering when you're going to achieve parity. She's wondering whether she should cross the street before she gets here. There she goes. Nice legs. Nice legs? You're one to speak. If there'd been any design changes in women in the past twenty years, you'd be the wrong person to ask about them. I think I'm a little more informed than that. Am I hurting you? You're hurting me. Not like a good woman would. A good woman would come between you and death. That would be about a temerarious vixen. I reiterate my earlier position. You mean I wouldn't even know the love of a good woman? You wouldn't even know the love of a bad woman. It has been a drought, of late. A dearth. A paucity. A veritable famine. Though doth calumniate me. Prove me wrong. This hip is hurting again. You're changing the subject. I'll need it to sprint after one, after all. One look at you, they'll rediscover the afterburner. You'll catch naught but phantoms. You're the phantom. How so? You saw her cross the street. There are both a bar and a taxi over there. You're demoted to the mere third possibility. At least she didn't roll us. She doesn't look the type. I reiterate my original position. I beg your pardon, but I *was* rolled by a woman, once. There you go, you must once have achieved parity. Otherwise I'd be dead. If we still had a news-paper in this town, we could check the obituaries. You don't fol-low the obituaries, the smart money intoned, they follow you. You're repeating yourself. Really? When did I ever say that— today, I mean. You shake your head. The only thing, the one thing, you were ever smart about was money. That's why…Yeah yeah yeah. If this hip gets any worse, it's going to take all day to get this rabbit's foot to the laundromat. Now you're talking about one of the big problems of the geriatricon. When the bog coughs up your mummy, will you still have your rabbit's foot? *Sans doute, mon frère. Le pied de lapin.* Good name for a bar. That *is* the name of that bar. Let's go in there, work on the old ethylcephalous condition. You mean the balance of martinis? The very same. You need money, to work on what you said. I thought we were chasing parity. Parity or women? That was a sad shake of the head. No money, no parity, no alcohol, no women. Chasing nothing. Pseudo-senility, this ain't. All too aware. Dementia in reverse. The floridity of your vegetative process. Confusion as regards sedulity. A calmative. Sip, rest, small talk. Sip, rest, small talk. A second drink, eventually. Soon enough, a skewing of the coronal plane. They're quite irresistible, martinis. Especially when you're old, out of work, trying to live long enough to achieve parity, when only a properly made martini is colder than you are. You're mighty opinionated, you say. I'm tired of staring at the barroom door, the smart money said. Having the economic wherewithal to make a stab at the pickling of ye perimysia in a civilized if extremely modest premises is one thing. Not having it is something else. Which is why you get the—. Which is why I'm bored with having been standing here on this bum hip for—what, half an hour?—staring at whatever modest premises…You're the one, who lost the walking stick. They're not irreplaceable. Not like the mind. That's rather an elevated opinion. Soon enough, soon enough… Can you tell where this is heading? *Le pied de lapin?* You're talking about a job, aren't you. No lamentation. A better suggestion, the smart money declares, though a long time coming, is always welcome. The note of challenge unmistakable. I fold my pair of tens. I think it's sevens.

TWO

IN THE MOVIES, I'M TOLD, GUYS ON THE WAY TO A JOB DO IT against what they call a bed of music. It doesn't work that way with me. Not that I can remember, anyway. If the moviemakers—my dictionary tells me that moviemaker is an acceptable compound; it's nice to feel acceptable once in a while, it's like finding an ort of succulent *lardon* in your gruel; and like that bit of flavor, you don't want to overdo it; another acceptable compound; *boatwright*, on the other hand, is not acceptable; and there you have it, the entire twenty-first century, in a nutshell, which is yet another unacceptable compound—want you to think you're right there, in the guy's head, identifying with his point view, he'll be wearing earbuds, an accepted compound not yet in printed dictionaries, maybe even squinting at the screen of his personal digital device as the French horns on the Gill Evans track thunder out of the surround-sound. Hm, what's with these guys, that's not an acceptable compound, even when hyphenated. This is what I hear, anyway, or imagine, at this point, since I don't talk to other people hardly at all, unless they want to discuss acceptable compounds in some kind of sensible manner, and not, as one fellow made the mistake of doing, waste my time with an off-color quip about my being an obstetrician. Off-color is an acceptable hyphenated compound. How do I know this, you may ask? What's a personal digital assistant for, if not as a tool to assist a person's awareness of his native language? The French horns of Gill Evans, may be a sensible response. But it's been a long time since I had to scoop fishheads—another unaccepted compound—and scale-flecked slush out of the hold of a purse seiner at Fisherman's Wharf—all wharf and no fishermen, these days, for one thing—but the smart money learnt me a better way to make a living. It's an excellent mode, too, episodic, finite, well-paid, cash on the nail under the table, so as not to interfere with the potential drip of Social Security checks. Scooping fishheads and scaled-flecked slush out of the holds of purse seiners was episodic, too, but it never paid well and, while you're actually pursuing it, it takes on all the aspects of a sordid infinity. And before I know it, me and the smart money find ourselves immediately behind the job, which is walking down the street minding its own business, if talking to somebody nobody else can see counts as business. I don't know, the job is saying as I get warm, really, what's the difference between apathy and ignorance? I don't know and I don't care! the smart money responded aloud, but the job doesn't hear the response because he is listening to some other response, and in any case neither response seems to affect him one way or another. It seems clear enough that he is waiting for what or whomever is on the other end of his earbuds to wind up this diversion so they can get back to business. Dude, he abruptly is saying, my 401(k) is like, ripped. I didn't give it to you to get it ripped. I gave it to you to grow. So I could retire in a timely and comfortable fashion. Now I'm going to have to, like, work until I'm a hundred and two. That's a good thing, the smart money pointed out, because there's very little extra space under that bridge abutment. Dude, the job is saying, you're not hearing what

I'm telling you, you gotta pay me back for your unfortunate misjudgment. You think I gave you my 401(k) to go to school on? I did not. That's what college is for. Don't you broker types go to college? Don't you all go to the same college? You hear me. That's right. You can't fool me. I know you went to college, and I could probably come to within a hundred-mile radius of where you went to college, because if you hadn't gone to college within that hundred mile radius the government wouldn't have bailed out your stupid mother-fucking brokerage house and if you take that other call I'm gonna take a cab downtown and kick you in the balls. Wait a minute, somebody's trying to tell me something. Snap, the smart money tells him. And down he goes in a flutter of ear-buds. Despite which trauma, he clings to his communications device. The smart money and I keep walking and it's easy because, as you know, nobody notices old people. Chicks, especially, they just look right through an elder person, sir or madame, unless they happen to be among the handful of movie stars who affect gray hair. Some pigeons will recognize the elderly, of course, if they're lovingly trained with day-old bread. The pigeons, not the elderly. Funny there was no blood. Just the earbuds. I turn the corner at the end of the block and the job is effectively over. The sun shines brightly in San Francisco today. But the streets are still fairly deserted, a symptom of the upper-case D Depression of '09, O'Dear. Eighty years between Depressions. One thinks about these things. None of the economists bloviating about this one is old enough to have experienced the last one. My dad was raised on a cotton farm in South Carolina. He was twelve in 1929. He told me they raised almost everything they needed on the farm and traded for the rest. A wagon would come across the river once a week and they would trade with it. A huge truck garden overrun with tomatoes (*Lycopersicon esculen-tum*) all summer long. Tomatoes are new world, you know. Spanish tomate, as well as tomatillo (*Physalis ixocarpa*, different but also new world), but I mention them to make a point, come from the Nahuatl *tomatl*. What do ya think of them apples, quips the smart money. I don't know and I don't care, I responded. It's etymology, etymology turns my crank at the far end of life, it comes from *eutmon*, Greek, which means the true sense of a word. So there. It's an anagram for Et tu, mon, almost, says the smart money, it's more or less— what Caesar said to Brutus, I interrupted, putatively said to him anyway, from the Latin for prune. At the light I take a right and cross the street, job putatively over. A pigeon swoops down, not ten yards away, and back up. For a minute there, I think it, the pigeon, recognized me. Didn't the Aztecs surrender to the Spanish in Nahuatl, which the Spanish transcribed, wonders the smart money. So it would appear, I says to him. That pigeon was an unusual color. That's true, says the smart money, white shot through with flecks of black on the body and wings, but dark gray on bluish black at the neck and tail feathers. One leg. You see that a lot. Why do you ask. It seems to me that we've seen this pigeon before. Achieving the middle of the block I jaywalk against traffic. An antique F Line street car rang its bell at me. One of the ones from Philadelphia, I believe. Achieving the curb, I maintain my direction, east, on the other side of Market Street. You'll recall that Elmo never jaywalked without his aluminum walker, the smart money observes. And he still got run over, I remind him. Elmo got run over? The smart money was suddenly all befuddled. But then the fog lifts and he says, oh yeah. I remember now. After they got him disentangled from that truck chassis, they had to cut him out of the aluminum tubes with the jaws of life. For all the good it did him. Yeah. Too bad they didn't cut George Bush out of his own aluminum tubes with the jaws of retirement. Man, snaps the smart money, are you never going to let that one go? It, be, like, later, now—you, know? Oh, I forgot, I declaim lamely, you're the fiscal conservative. He had *bad intell*, the smart money insisted. Now who's not letting it go? I pointed out. That guy over there. Where? At the cable car turnaround. And there, beyond the chess players, an electric blues guitarist, two mimes and a long line of people obviously from somewhere else, sit an elderly couple in nylon-webbed aluminum lawn chairs, green warp and dirty white woof. More elderly than me? Naw, says the smart money, they just look it. It's all down to diet. Diet, and television. One holds a hand-lettered sign that declares, SarA PaliN Is A BabE. HoT. BRinG oN 2012. The other holds a sign that reads, Immigrant Go Home, in one hand; in another hand another sign reads, Marriage Is Between One Man And One Woman Before The Eyes Of God. How'd he get all that dense information on one sign? I wondered idly. The First Amendment, the smart money remarks, it makes me proud. Shall not we loiter near them? I suggest. Maybe the smell will drive them away. They'll just go to another cable car turnaround, the smart money says, hey mister, where you from? The man ignores us both. What's the matter? the smart money says, don't you know? Or does the question make you uncomfortable. Relax. You're in San Francisco. In San Francisco, everybody's from somewhere else. You been here five years? You qualify as a native. Hey, what's the difference between apathy and ignorance? Now the woman looks at us, adjusts her sunglasses, then nudges her husband. I don't know and I don't care, he says without looking at us. Go away. How can I go away? the smart money says, I live here. Ask him when's the last time he had a bath, the woman says to her husband. Madame, I stipulate, lofting to the altitude of my dignity, when George Bush the Second floated that horse-pucky about Saddam Hussein trying to buy aluminum tubes and uranium yellow cake from Nigeria on top of the supposed secret meeting in Czechoslovakia between the head of Iraqi Intelligence and Muhammad Atta buoyed in their turn by the mythological weapons of mass destruction, I quit bathing in protest. It worked, the woman says. You stink. Don't you just love the First Amendment? the smart money asks her. Not like the afore-listed horse pucky, Madame, stank and, I hasten to assure you, stinks, present tense. The woman frowns. Which one's that? she asks, her curiosity apparently overcoming her reluctance to speak to strangers. That's the one about free speech, the smart money replies. What we need, the husband abruptly expostulates, is the amendment about one man one woman. He let one of his signs droop in his lap, slogan up, as he covers his wife's hand with one of his own. Like us. Fiscal conservative or not, the smart money says, I think I'm gonna puke. A cable car arrives. Both mimes, the blues musician, and one of the chess players course up one side and down the other of the queue of tourists, each artist bearing an upturned hat or, in the case of one of the mimes, a George Bush lunch box. An ambulance, its siren easily 120 decibels, turns the corner at Montgomery Street, Dopplers past the cable car turnaround, deafening us all, and herds cars in front of itself until it can perform an illegal left turn onto Sixth Street. Two equally loud black and white police cars follow suit. And then a hook-and-ladder fire truck. Damn that's loud, the woman says after a moment. What'd you say? her husband asks, turning his head. Damn loud, she shouts into

his ear. Damn straight, he nods, even I heard it. I'm beginning to like these people, the smart money enthuses, they're
old *and* they're conservative. Pretty amusing, I agree. If I had
my portable tomography machine along with me, the smart
money lasciviates, I'd enlarge their respective *trigonum cere-
brae* just enough to make raving faggots out of both of them.
They'd still be married, the smart money adds. And they'd
still be conservative, I point out. Is there such a thing, is wondered aloud, as a conservative queer? Are you kidding me?
the smart money replies in kind, let's start with Roy Cohen
and J. Edgar Hoover. Why those hectoring homewreckers, I
reply archly. I hear you, the smart money says. What is he
saying about them great Americans, the man asks his wife. I
can't hear him for the smell, his wife replies. We're going to
be late, the smart money abruptly recollects. You got a point,
I reply. Sir or Madame, as the case may be, we bid you adieu.
Phew, the woman declares brusquely, riddance. As goes the
odor, so goeth the politics, I offer anodynely, and roll my eyes
skyward, look out for the giant California flies. Both of them
look up. Gotcha, says the smart money, and we take ourselves
away. Away being up Powell street, toward Union Square,
which is thronged as usual, including two additional mimes,
at least I think they are additional, a good thing I suppose,
not that I embrace benevolence, and, once arrived, sure
enough, nobody notices me ask a man if I could have the
newspaper he is about to throw into a trash can, because, as
I keep telling you, I'm sixty-three and therefore invisible. On
the contrary, people probably expect me to ask them for
things, any sort of thing, and they're relieved to see the pinch
fall upon another. He, on the other hand, refrains from jocu-
larly inquiring as to whether I want a newspaper to wipe my
ass with, as a man with a certain cut of jib might well have

thought to do, given the cut of my own jib. Certainly, he rather replies, sharing a newspaper amongst readers, plural, is a bloody green thing to do. I couldn't agree more, sirrah, I respond, taking the paper, and it will pass an old man's time most agreeably. Plainly then, he declares, you haven't read a word of it, else you'd revise that opinion, and with no more ado we go our separate ways, he down the steps at the northeast corner of the Square, debouching to the intersection of Stockton and Post Streets, and I to a bench facing south and the midday solar entity, beaming most friendly over the roof of Macy's, across Geary Street. Always the same bit with the newspaper, the smart money observes, never the same guy with the bit, and that's far and away the most conversation we've ever gotten out of any one of them. If you call it a conversation, I put in, my eyes closing against the sun. It really is warm, and I am over-ragged. I'm either going to have to remove a blanket or two, I think to myself, or I'm going to have to retreat to my chill cavity beneath the bridge abutment. Tonight we do without the hole, the smart money reminds me, unless we've been had. I forgot about that aspect of futurity, I admit, opening my eyes. Let's have a look. As Cities Go From Two Newspapers to One, Some Talk of Zero, a headline read. That's going to put a crimp in our style, the smart money suggests. Man, I point out, you are such a worry-wart. You think that's just them walking their solipsism? the smart money says, somewhat hopefully. That's exactly what I think, I reply, turning to the Sports section, from which I retrieve a thickly padded plain white envelope. Gives me the creeps, the smart money says, wondering who licked that. Maybe they use a damp sponge in a saucer, I suggest, you say that every time. So do you, the smart money says. It's the right thickness, I surmise, and squirrel the envelope into a slit in my rags. It will be five grand in filthy C-notes. I don't count it. If we were to do this every two weeks, the smart money says, we could afford to live in San Francisco. Yeah, I point out, but then we'd have tax problems. I wonder where they get all those dirty hundreds. Religious Leaders Fight Bill to Open Abuse Cases. Same old, same old. I turn a page. Damn, lookit that anaconda. Probably the last one, the smart money says.

THREE

So you're in the bar with your $5000. It's a bar you know intermittently well, the intermittence in direct relation to how the work goes, they make their martinis very cold in there, and this is how they do it. The ice, the glass, the cocktail shaker and the bottle of gin and/or vodka (we're not going to get into a pissing match about what constitutes a real martini, are we?) are kept in a freezer. Everything else—olives, vermouth, even the toothpicks—are kept in a refrigerator. First, the shaker is removed from the freezer. It's better that the top of the shaker and its vessel are separated, as they are rinsed with cold water while in transit from dishwasher to freezer, otherwise the unit will have to thaw a bit, after freezing, before they are able to be separated and thus, by the delay, accrue deleterious calories. As a concession to intimacy as opposed to alcoholism, no more than two martinis are conceived simultaneously. Vermouth is dispensed from a spritzer of the kind you'd mist your pitcher plants with (*Sarracenia, Nepenthes,* or *Darlingtonia,* they're all cool), and one or two spritzes, so as to mist the wall of the cocktail shaker opposite the user, and no more, are quite sufficient, particularly if you're drinking high-end vodka or gin, which products declaim otherwise definite opinions vis-à-vis the net flavor of their constituent herbals. In fact, if you're spending more than one hundred dollars on your fifth of vodka and particularly your gin, you might want to dispense altogether with your vermouth. In the event, however, only dry vermouth will do, never a sweet one. It's important to remember the origin of the martini, which derives from the American era of Prohibition (1919-1933: can you believe it?), whence arose the necessity of masking the flavor of bathtub gin. Hence, in researching the recipes of the era, at the San Francisco Public Library, one will discover the startling admonition to mix one's martini in the ratio of two parts gin to one part vermouth, an admonition unthinkable, nearly a hundred years later, in an era of, in fact, the hundred dollar bottle of gin into whose flavor some chemist has devoted a career of experimentation and taste, which holds true for all but the lowest rotgut—a compound with which we have learnt to live—product available from your corner ghetto grocery. And, a piece of advice from the smart money? You can turn rotgut vodka into entirely acceptable cocktail material with an inexpensive, home-built charcoal filtration system. Be that as it may, do not let such stray thoughts deviate you from building the perfect martini. Spritz with dry, chilled vermouth, as I was saying, the far wall of the frozen canister, once or twice is enough. Drop in three or four cubes of ice; better, two scoops of cracked ice; crushed ice will work if everything is properly chilled and celerity is not sacrificed to a phone call or a text message. Next, enter vodka or gin sufficient to fill your cocktail glass(es), judging which quantity only practice will perfect. Cover and shake vigorously. None of your pussified shaking, shake vigorously. If the shaker is stainless steel (do not use an aluminum cocktail shaker, or a plated one, as the constituent metals may aggravate the infantilization already brought on by excessive alcohol consumption) and the ingredients have been properly conditioned, the shaker may well numb your hand, your hand may even become frozen to it.

Be tough. Separate your hand from the metal, which should frost nicely, like a windshield in Chicago in January. Let stand. Meanwhile, remove olives and toothpicks from the refrigerator, spear two of the former with one of the latter, remove one frozen martini glass from the freezer and drop the garnish into it. Immediately take up the shaker and vigorously shake as before. The touch of the frosted stainless steel to the fingers and palm of your hand should by now be painful. Persevere. Experience will teach you how long to prolong this second shake. Now pour, shaking the cocktail shaker as you do so. This should result in shards of ice garnishing the volume as well as the surface of the cocktail, to the extent that, just rattling the last of the driblets out of the shaker, the volume of the martini is shot through with filaments as in some polar febrile dream, and its surface should have a skim of slush atop it. Taste. An expostulation should be readily available. And there I was, between that first sip, when the conic beaker is too full to move or to touch, other than with envacuumating lips, and my first expostulation, when a guy sits down next to me and says, "Did you hear the one about George Bush getting evicted from the White House?" I didn't even answer the guy. George Bush has been out of office for—what, a year? Five years? Ten? I lost track. I skim the second blast off the top of this gelid martini, maybe two molecules deep, half vodka and half ice crystals, they only make such martinis in one bar in all of San Francisco, where they call such a drink the Apsley Cherry-Garrard, and it's so cold my lips turn black with frostbite and my larynx turns to permafrost, so I can't answer the guy anyway. "They couldn't get him out," the guy says, "because he was caught between Iraq and a hard place." He slaps the bar. "Get it? Iraq and a hard place?" The bartender, whose name is Gerrold, points at the door. "Get out," he says. "What?" the guy says, "you some kind of Republican?" "No," Gerrold replies, "I'm a publican, and I'm cutting you off." "But I haven't even had so much as a single drink," the customer complains. "You're disturbing my best customer," Gerrold says. "Who," the guy says, "this bum?" I don't care, I'm into my third sip now. My chin is only maybe an inch off the bar, not counting whiskers, my lips couldn't have been more extruded toward the rim of the martini glass if they'd been on the flatulating southbound end of a northbound jackass. "That's right," Gerrold says. He tapped the bar with a forefinger. "My best fucking customer." "But what about the smell?" the citizen protests. "The color of his money cancels his odor without prejudice," the publican declares. "It's like having a cushion between your ass and a bed of nails." The rim of the cocktail glass is like a knife easing laterally through the crease between my lips. It's a wound, a stigma of devotion almost, a holy aperture, and, while you know, you can't feel. The only sound is of the last slurp of a bilgepump felching a limber hole. But it's not the last. "That's impressive," the citizen admits. "How about I buy him a drink, he looks like he needs the boost, and we forget my little indiscretion and make a drink for me, too." "Up to him," Gerrold says. "My name's Marty." The citizen offers a hand. I show him mine. The guy visibly winces. I shrug and sip. The hand is still filthy from when, while mulling my algebra, I absently masturbated the besooted rabbit's foot. The martini's gone down enough to move the glass now, so I reposition it onto a fresh napkin, right in front of me, and hunch down on the stool like a shitting ape. The conversation diminishes into the background. You should try to be more sociable, the smart money mentions. You've mentioned that before, I point out. Yeah, but it's getting worse, you know. Pretty soon they might not even let you in here. That would be a shame, I say, with a loving look at the martini. As it is, they make certain allowances. You should come in here after you clean up. It's only after I come in here, I remind him, that I can face getting cleaned up. I know it's easier to maintain your degradation than to go through it all over again, the smart money responds, and it's true, he's put his mouth on the pulse of the matter, a sensation one experiences but rarely. "He seems to be in some kind of holy state," the citizen says from far away, but not so far that I can't hear him. "You might have something there," Gerrold says. "On the other hand," the citizen reflects, "he might just be an alcoholic bum." "I would rather you modify your tone," Gerrold tells him. "Gladly," replies the citizen, "so long as you serve me a drink." He looks one way, then another. "There are only but the two customers in here, taking myself into account." Let the man have his drink, the smart money suggests. "That'll be a Guinness," the citizen says. "But I'll take it down here," and he moves to the far end of the bar. You'd think one look at you and a man would be fed up with drink, the smart money observed. More's the pity, I say to him, you can lead a citizen to the blackboard but you can't make him dust. There's something to that, the smart money allows. Then perhaps you'll be so kind as to explain it to me, I reply. It's a real twister, the smart money ponders. It's precisely dust that you or he or someone at any rate but in the end, one way or another, life itself will make of him. Dust. Precisely, I tell him. Dust precisely. "How about them 'Niners?" the citizen at the bar says after he's had a sip. "Think they got a chance?" There's barm on his upper lip. Gerrold sighs as loud as a man can sigh without flapping his lips injuriously. "Listen," Gerrold says, "you've paid good money to sit in this bar and drink in peace, as did this other fellow, here." He indicates me, of all people. Fellow implies peer, and I bristle. "Can't you leave well enough alone?" "But I'm concerned," the citizen, Marty, says. "What if they don't make the playoffs?"

33

"I'd be more concerned if they did make the playoffs," Gerrold interpolates. "Why?" the citizen says. "Because then I'd have to listen to any number of silly fucks like yourself," replies Gerrold, "instead of just the one." "Am I to suppose," the citizen declares with sufficient incredulity, "that I'm the only person in this establishment who gives a shit about the 'Niners?" Gerrold looks at him. "It's one-third of the population," he says. "Don't you think that's enough?" "What's the 'Niners?" the smart money astutely injects. "What?" Incredulity elevates the brow of the citizen to new height. "What?" he flusters. "Is it an agglutination of endeavor, the sole purpose of which is to advance the oblate token of pseudo-nationalism from one end of a screen to the other?" "Say," concludes Gerrold, somewhat gleefully, "that might well be the 'Niners." "Organized sports pave the road to fascism," the smart money postulates darkly. The citizen's gob waxes, smacked. "I have a phone," he finally says. "I could report you." "To whom, and for what offense," the smart money demands, deploying a tone, it is true, of pseudo-incredulity. "To Homeland Security," the citizen replies without hesitation, "for unpatriotic fervor." "And the result?" the smart money sneers. "Whatever time you spend in confinement," the citizen replies with no hesitant uncertainty, "will be well-compensated by loud and unceasing broadcast of football and other, akin, behavioralisms. Country music, for just one example." "Until you cry uncle," Gerrold whispered timorously. "That would be correct," the citizen replied. But, sensing his moral superiority, he allowed his voice to snarl, and gave his lip to ostentate a ready sneer. "Better you than me," Gerrold turns to me and says. But I'm now drinking the martini with an actual hand motion, bending of the elbow. And it's not judiciously I'm drinking it. One two three, maybe a fourth sip, and the glass is pushed aside empty, keep the olives, and the knuckle is rapped on the winter grain of the plank, in hopes of a wintry riposte, in the form of the second Apsley Cherry-Garrard. A word about olives. They should be of the small, Manzanilla type, pitted and stuffed with a scrap of pimento. Some like their martini "dirty", with a bit of the fluid packing the olives in their jar adduced to the cocktail, and the connection is well-named but, one man's linoleum floor is another man's ceiling and, by extreme metaphorical extension, his vision of upper-case G God or H Hell, as the case may be, life is too short to adjudicate errant tastes; although of course the contra-positive of that homily is the more forceful admonition that, either you adjudicate the tastes of others, or they will endeavor to adjudicate yours. Is not that the foundation of all human earnestness? I ask you, the smart money says. As go dirty martinis, cf. viz. vermouth, above, I reply; but, and I blink: did not I ask you first? No, the smart money returns smoothly, it had something to do with the apostrophe upper-case N 'Niners. I shake my inner head gravely. I think not, I think not me, I think not I, I think not that I have ever let the word 'Niners escape my lips, lo these sixty-odd years. Nor has any of my nominative pronouns. Not once. Surely, the smart money elides urbanely, you have never so much as discussed the Gold Rush? I shiver my jowls until my wattle quivers. Indignation, I respond with dignity, is my sole remaining vehicle of transport. What if the top line of your email suddenly goes black with refreshment? postulates the smart money. Do you not quicken? Gerrold, I telepath aloud, your martiniless environment heaps me. "Last year they went ten and six. It sucked, man. I'm telling you, I was ready to kill myself." Gerrold, I telepath, what are you going to countenance next? Autonecrophilia? "The salary cap hamstringed the entire club," the citizen continues. Hamstrung, I wince. Hamstrung the entire club foot. The smart money shakes the head. It's like a rattle on a stick. So many puns, so much money. "Smith said it was not a blow to the ego to take a large pay cut after making $26.3 million over the first four years of his contract." The smart money sighs the sigh of deep, of profound enervation. With a rattle of sharp-edged cubes and by the light of the ancient Olympia waterfall, the shaker twinkles high over Gerrold's head. "No key injuries reported," the citizen says, between ineffectual flicks of his tongue at the ridge of barm on his upper lip. Finally, he drags a sleeve over the foam and says, "I don't believe what the front office is putting out there." "If the agora had been as rife with intell about Iraq as it is with factoids about the 'Niners' locker room," Gerrold has the temerity to point out, "we might not have to be facing the present-tense karma of the second Bush administration." "It's hard to discuss politics with the patriotic," the smart money put in. "What Smith really wants to do is not change teams," the citizen continues, "but stick with the club in order to prove to them they haven't invested in his future in vain." "But they fucked with his contract," Gerrold suddenly blurts. Gerrold, the smart money telepaths, do your job. And as if by the miracle of telekinesis, Gerrold sets down the shaker, revealing a perfect handprint in its frosted carapace, and spears a couple of olives while saying, as if to them, "But his contract was based on his starting at least half the games in the season, and there's a reversion clause if he doesn't," revealing an incredible ability to multitask, while, suffused with relief, despite Gerrold's apparent hypocrisy, the smart money soothes my neurasthenia. The thing about the Manzanilla olives, the smart money is saying, projecting through the miasma of a near migraine, is that they take up only a fraction of the volume of vodka or gin in the martini that those big ones do. It seems pretty obvious that, given that your basic olive is a prolate spheroid, its volume is determined by the expression

$$V = 4/3 \times \pi \times a^2 \times b$$

where

$$a = \text{horizontal transverse radius}$$

and

$$b = \text{vertical conjugate radius}$$

then, given these here pimento-stuffed Manzanilla olives (*Olea europa pomiformis*)

$$a = 3/8"$$
$$b = 1/2"$$

and so,

$$V = 4/3 \times \pi \times (3/8)^2 \times 1/2 = .09375 \text{ cubic inches}$$

which, times two olives per martini equals 0.1875 cubic inches per martini. As opposed to the volume of one of those big green olives, where

$$a = 3/4"$$
$$b = 1"$$

and so,

$$V = 0.75 \text{ cubic inches}$$

which, times two, equals 1.5 cubic inches. Not to mention, they're completely tasteless and so green as in unfermented as to utterly resist the admonitions of the average set of public assistance dentures. So the difference between the two is

$$1.5 \text{ cubic inches} - 0.1875 \text{ cubic inches} = 1.3125 \text{ cubic inches}$$

which cooks down to an incredible 0.727125 fluid ounces of vodka or gin—half a jigger! And Gerrold knows this. Gerrold lands the martini on a fresh napkin—never a coaster—in front of me. It's brimful. Bacilli-like filaments swarm through the clear fluid. It's topped by five millimeters of slush. Two modest volumes of olives dangle, speared by an as-yet-to-be-calculated volume of toothpick, but the sliver of balsa may be just enough to lend negative buoyancy to the discrete little fruit, we'll wait for the third one to essay the algebra, it's colder than Apsley Cherry-Garrard on the Ross ice shelf in August, that's the southern, polar August, its cruelest month. And so, in short, I take a sip, and today, now, as of this moment, nobody else has to die.

FOUR

THE ONE SURE THING ABOUT BINGE DRINKING IS THAT SOONER or later, while you know you're going to wake up under that bridge abutment again, the question is whether you're going to wake up there in one piece. You're going to open your eyes quite abruptly. There may be sunlight. There may be flies. The wall of plastic bags caught in the chain link fence may be rustling in a slight breeze. There may be the usual regret, that you didn't spend some of that five thousand dollars on a tetanus shot, or Stress B supplements, rather than two weeks in an SRO hotel and the vodka delivery system known as the martini, otherwise known as the oblivion package. When you are younger you can handle this sort of abuse—when you were younger, you did handle this sort of abuse. The miracle and the curse are the same, that you somehow survived long enough to where it really hurts, it is really damaging, it is terminally detrimental to your health. You're surrounded by other people who are doing more or less the same thing to themselves. Some of them are genuinely crazy, of course. They've been driven mad by war, poverty, actuality, reality, compromise, women, men, children, gods, the snipped off end of a price tag in the collar of a shirt they wore for years, television, the lottery they never won, the lottery they did win, the mercury poisoning they got from a diet of clams and thermometers, robocalls, junk faxes, the repossession of their home, the loss of a job they had for 35 years, the death of a beloved pet, the laundry room in a sub-basement of The Four Seasons Hotel, cutting compound miters on thousands of 20 gauge 2x6 steel studs, lingerie catalogues—like that. It doesn't help that almost everybody out here is aware that their fillings receive every frequency of broadcast signal. While cellphone transmission has only made the fill-ceiver situation worse, most of us feel that, since cellphones have ostensibly normal people as if talking to themselves, thus providing some cover for the truly schizophrenic, the playing field has leveled somewhat. But the smart money knows the location of every unguarded power outlet in San Francisco, and often makes a buck by revealing one location or another to some homeless person stupid enough to be needing to charge the cellphone they need in order to keep in touch with whomever it is abuses them the most. Another upside is that cellphones have made it much easier to arrange deals for drugs, stolen goods, etc. The smart money actually knows a guy called Upside. Why do they call him Upside? He works like this. One day Upside was sitting on a rock rolling a cigarette when a tourist said, "Excuse me, sir, but I'm trying to find my way to Fisherman's Wharf." Now, Upside knew that he could have thrown the rock he was sitting on and hit Jefferson Street, which is the southern terrestrial border of Fisherman's Wharf. Upside knew he might even tap the tourist for a buck after the exchange of information, leaving the assholism on the tourist's chit if he declined to help him out. But Upside doesn't look on the upside. Hence his name. What Upside chose to do was lock onto the tourist with his mirror shades, like they were the binocular cross hairs of his nose cannon. It was a warm day in San Francisco, and the tourist had his jacket hooked on a finger and slung over his shoulder. He, too, had on a pair of shades. But he did not possess no nose cannon. "I don't give a shit," Upside suddenly yelled at the guy, "I just lost all my clothes." "Oh," said the startled tourist, while managing to add, "Well, you still have your tobacco." Upside took a drag, as if considering this feel-good optimism— although, in fact, feel-good optimism is one of his pet peeves. At length he held the cigarette slightly away from his face, exhaled smoke at it. "I don't give a fucking damn," he announced. "Okay, okay," the tourist said, backing away, adding, "Have a nice day," as he walked away. People who passive-aggressively try to get in the last word are another of Upside's pet peeves. When the tourist had managed to put about twenty yards between them, Upside yelled, "Why don't you find your dick and shove it up your ass!" That's why we call him Upside. If a situation can be made worse, he's your man. Or you are, puts in the smart money. Don't fuck with my hangover, I remind the smart money. If we're going to play it like that, responds the smart money, you're going to be one lonely son of a bitch. Don't use that tone with me this morning, I advised the smart money, because if you do, I might start killing people for free. I thought we had a deal, came the reply, after a short silence. And another thing, I declare, no more of these pregnant pauses. I want *rapid-fire patter*. You hear what I'm saying? I hear what you're saying. There came a prolonged silence. What did I just say to you? *Rapid-fire patter.* What about it? It takes two. And I suppose the hangover is the problem. No, it's the drinking that's the problem. There was a time, a body found itself at a loss for words? Yes? A body took a shower. Or stripped down and jumped into the Pacific. Or went jogging, worked up a sweat. Don't come the acid with me, young fella. And where do you see a shower, a Pacific, or beatable feet? No place whatsoever. But the Pacific is about six miles thataway. Toward the sunset. Away from the sunrise. It is bright. You lost those shades? That would appear to be the case. You make it hard for a body to present its case. Since when do sunglasses present

a case? How much money do we have left? None. Not a dime?
Not a centime. Please directly address the absent or imaginary
person or personified abstraction. Help yourself. You clear your
throat of a good bolus, hawk it downwind with authority, and
your stomach almost goes with it. What's the name of that
Hawaiian fish, you ask aloud, that pukes its internal organs when
threatened? As go digressions that's a good start. Nobody's threat-
ening you. Five thousand dollars, up in smoke, one might seek
five thousand more, were it not a trope. Hangovers always make
you rhyme. Son of a bitch, expostulated the smart money, find
your dick and stick it up your ass. You left my dick in Phoenix,
I said sadly. Oh no, don't start in on her, the smart money
bemoaned, not only because it was twenty-five years ago, and not
only because no matter how you remember it you won't remember it accurately, but in the main because, if you were to somehow find the woman in question, she wouldn't remember it at all.
If there been any design changes in women, I agreed. You'd be
the last person from whom to seek information concerning them,
the smart money finished. It's when visions of sugar plums begin
to dance in my head, I led out. That you most wish for full-time,
mind-dulling employment. A double whammy, I agreed. Like
war. I'm at war. I suppose that's true. I get paid to be at war.
Incredible that you figured that out. Find a hole and fill it, I
always say. I couldn't abide dentistry. If you countenanced more
latitude in your attitude you might have learnt to tune amalgam,
for but one suggestion. What with all the people out here in the
real world receiving way too many signals by means of their fillings, you'd never be out of work. This isn't working, I abruptly
state. I need less technology than I already have, not more. What
technology is it, that you need less of? The technology of self-
awareness. You're too sensitive, the smart money guessed. I
believe that it's you, who, more than once, have been accused of

condescension. Exquisite condescension, the smart money qual-
ified. Condescension is an art form. Fuckem, if they can't take a
joke. I do not jape, nor cajole—in a word, I am not a cage to be
lured into. Not like the Niners. That's a fact. The road to fascism
is paved with pass completions and pass interceptions. Equally.
Now we're talking. It's about time. It seems like it's taken all
morning. It's hard to get started, lacking aspirin. Painful. It's like
replacing one obscenity with another, fuck, say, with sheetrock.
Or vice versa. As I was saying. What do you have against sheetrock? Martian vistas. That's it? Can you see the mental shrug?
Completely mental. Too short. The mouth tastes like a vole
(*Microtus*) slept in it. You might have come up with a new sim-
ile, after all these years. How many? Close on to fifty, I'd say.
Since we heard that bit about the vole? I'd say. They should put
that on your tombstone. I'd say? You'd say. Not condescension as
an art form? Exquisite condescension. Not *Ici vecu de 1928 a sa
mort La Capitaine Dreyfus 1859 - 1935*? He lived that long? So
it would seem. There's a guy who got hosed. Yes. It reminds me
of the day you helped Sinbad bind up that head wound. Head
wound, head wound…It was a while back. Years. You know how
a head wound bleeds. There was blood all over the place. He was
so dazed he didn't know whether he'd been whacked or fallen
down, let alone in possession of the wherewithal to hold a com-
press to the wound. So you helped him. Cleaned him up a bit.
You always carried a canteen full of vodka, in those days. A shame
to waste it on a head wound, but one does what one can. Point
being? Point being it was an hour before you got back to finish-
ing those potato chips. You were sitting on the sea wall on the
north side of the parking lot next to the St. Francis Yacht Club,
watching a big freighter head out the Golden Gate, yourself
being watched by a Western gull (*Larus occidentalis*), as you
gradually became aware that the hand with which you were eat-

ing the chips out of the bag had not been washed since you bound up the wound on Sinbad, who, as you recall, in a fit of delirium tremens the last time you'd seen him under the bridge, had happened to mention that he'd tested positive for the human immunodeficiency virus, which is commonly spread by…you look at the handful of potato chips…blood contact. There came a long pause. So this is how it ends, you think like a Jay McInerney character. Do you really want to give a single thought, at the beginning of the end of your life, to Jay McInerney? You crush the chips in your fist like they're gold and you're Fred C. Dobbs, and there's no water to trade it for. That's probably not an apt pair of similes, but you're improving. Awk, says the Western gull, and it raises both wings in gratitude or in self-defense as you scatter the handful of chips along the top of the seawall, and another, bigger gull lands immediately, its echoing plaint barely audible to you, full of wonder as you are as to how frayed the far end of your twine has turned out to be. But you don't give it the whole bag, because that size is almost four dollars now. No, you roll it up and tuck it into the hood of hooded Niners sweatshirt they gave you at the foodbank the day before yesterday, and you step down to the water's edge and wash your hands in the chill waters of the San Francisco Bay. Bleach, you think. Why am I not under the bridge abutment, where the smart specie always clean their syringes with bleach between uses? Many of them enjoy to watch a syringe as it spurts straight up. A sign you live, as it were. Delight the wellspring of the future. It says so on the door of the yoga studio. For the time being, sea water will have to do. Down there, along the beachfront, a half-mile away, is a public rest-room, maybe with hot water. In the opposite direction, down Bay Street, along the Marina Green, through the doglegs of the park-ing lot cozening Gas House Cove, past Fort Mason, up one hun-dred steps and over the cypress-shaded hill to Aquatic Park, past

the Maritime Museum, there's another public restroom, close
aboard the Dolphin Club, right before you get to the Hyde Street
Pier. It, too, might have hot water. A little further along, down
Jefferson Street and up Taylor to Bay, there's a Safeway, where
you might have purchased a bottle of bleach, if you had had any
money, which gets us back to the seawall next to the St. Francis
Yacht Club and the canteen nowhere near full of vodka, and for
the second time in a day you called on the vodka for its antisep-
tic, rather than its analgesic, property. What is a substance with
anti-analgesic, pain-inducing properties, if not throe-inducing,
and hence, right away, without tarry, we come to he who craves
or indeed offers, sells, procures pain, the throe-monger. Once I
was President. Oh yes, there's a woman under the bridge who
calls herself the First Woman President, or Madame President,
for short. A pity, as you watch it trickle over the palm of the the-
oretically afflicted hand, and redoubled sufficient to scrub the
two hands together, and trebled as an equivalent dose makes its
way down the gullet, but easy come and easy conceived, as my
mother used to say, a harridan, in short, scolding and vicious and
well out of it, lo these many fiscal years. And that'll be enough of
that memory, a total scatological construct by now at any rate, at
this distance you can scarcely recall the sound of her voice,
although the odor of a mildewed and remaindered non-fiction
novel allows something of her essence to spring to mind, a his-
tory of the Dreyfus affair, for instance, the outbound freighter
has been replaced by an inbound one, and, now the hands have
been cleansed, out comes the bag of potato chips along with a
question, to wit: does the priest, having masturbated, wash his
hands before mass? Any more, for that matter, than he flogs himself with a length of barbed wire? I think not. Hot and cold running water in the sacristy is on the to-do list. Two more reasons
not to attend upper-case M Mass, the not-to-do list is endless.

Just the other day the Pope expressed himself quite well on the subject, proclaiming the use of prophylactics as contributing to the spread of HIV virus rather than its containment. There you go again, pal, enticing the masses into the cage, there to fester along with their beloved Niners forever. Listen, man, I told you, don't be getting so worked up. You got a point, you told me, and you filled your mouth with potato chips. Now wash that down with some vodka. Yassuh. And, excepting this existential heart attack, the day passed as it should. Nobody died, for example, at least not within your immediate perimeter. Least of all the Pope. His time will come, as yours nearly did. That was something, wasn't it. I imagine it was. If only you could remember it. If only I could remember it. How the revelation did seep through your very cellular structure, that, in giving aid to your fellow man, you might verily perhaps have sealed your own kismet. That would be ironic, to say the least, to see a man who has spent his entire adult life trying to die of natural causes, and that sooner than later, somehow persevering to the point of meeting his death by the hand of charity. Your waxing conceptual, here. Eliding, more like it. From potato chips to the Pope to the bridge abutment to the sea, from one public restroom to the west, to another to the east, pulverized by indecision, incapable of discerning the moral relativity of one bathroom over the other, unless you take into account that the one more likely to have hot water is exactly twice as far away as the one less likely to dispense hot water, and so if you take a chance on the shorter walk and discover the hot water to be nonexistent there, you'll wind up walking two miles instead of half a mile to your goal, and is this what they call ethical subjectivism? Or are the two bathrooms and their possibilities a prime example of value pluralism? It seems to me, says the smart money, that what we have here is a prime example of the exquisite condescension of upper case G God, relative to the human condition. If you were in any other world theater, Bangladesh, for example, and presumably having no resources whatsoever as regards your personal hygiene, whereas if at your age you weren't long dead already, you would eat the potato chips and the HIV virus be damned, as, for one excellent point, by the time AIDS kills you something else would already have accomplished the deed long since. So what's good for the goose is good for the gander? No, no, not at all. Rather, it's very much akin to the accommodation you've reached with your penchant for killing people who offend you. How so? Well, you've managed to contain the impulse at least to the extent of getting paid for what you, sooner or later, will not be able to restrain yourself from doing. That's true. True? It's brilliant. Thank you. But if you're following my logic here, what if the flag were to be hung one day, you picked up the package, the photo turned out to be that of a young woman, and, in the event, the young woman turned out to be a nursing mother. Then what? That's an excellent question. I presume what you're driving at is, should the baby be done in with its mother, since, without her, it will find itself pretty much done in, in terms of suffering at least, if not in terms of life outright, anyway? Is that what you're driving at? You are coming on like an odious creature, but yes. I don't know, to tell you the truth. But, since I am inclined not to do my fellow hominid any favors...You see where I'm going. The frailty of life, the helplessness of a fellow mortal, these mean nothing to you. No more than their strength or power. So, let's see, let's say you were a feminist. Were? I am a feminist. Okay, you're a feminist. Now, let's further suppose you are an anti-interventionist. What the hell is that? Well, let's say that your country has become hopelessly mired in the politics, cultural mores, and ethical byways of some other country. Afghanistan, for example? Afghanistan, for example. Yeah. Afghanistan, for example, where girls can't go to school, and if they do, they get acid thrown in their face. But that's their culture. Somebody's culture, anyway. Yes. So it's not a secular world, it's a religious one. Religiously controlled. Okay. What about it? Is it your position as a feminist that girls in this country should be allowed to go to school, despite it's being culturally unacceptable, just because they would be allowed to go to school in your country? More like, just because they go to school in my century. Interesting point. Yeah. Trans-eonic. An eon contains two or more eras. Oh yeah. Okay, let's narrow it down some. Let's. Let's look at it that, because of the evolved technology in your era, you have managed to launch and land your heavily armed time machine in that other country's other era. And there they are, in their era, throwing acid into the faces of girls who dare to go to school. What do you do? Ahm, get back in my time machine and go back to my own era? Probably a good idea. Unless you want to grapple with a whole other era. Yeah. A whole other era. Let's take it a step further. Okay. What if they have oil in that era? Petroleum. Uh, hold them at gunpoint and take their oil and fill up the tank on the time machine and ship it back to our era? Sure, why not. They'd probably be fine with that, so long as you didn't try to make them let their girls go to school while you were at it. That's probably correct. Okay, what if some girl came up and begged you to take her back to your era. That would probably depend on what she looked like, and whether or not I were heterosexual. What if she told you that if you left her behind they were going to throw acid in her face just for talking to you, just as soon as you left. You're messing with my mood, here, I feel that I'm getting grumpy just trying to parse all this horseshit. Bear with me. Bear with you? I'm stuck with you for life.

FIVE

WORKING UNDER THE TABLE IS ALWAYS THE PROBLEM, WHEN
you're getting Social Security. It's hard to work under the table
when there's a mortgage on your bridge abutment. Banks tend
to keep records, and that's why their under-the-table depositors
get into trouble from time to time. But on the whole, bankers
come out ahead. Oh, you noticed that. I noticed that. Show me
a banker. Can't, they're all disguised, these days. You would
think one of them would sneak up on me and take his revenge.
And why would one want to do that? Why, because you are the
one who so front-burners, so makes a display of, his effrontery,
his success, his Mercedes 650 SL. This pair of little wheels sup-
porting my hind end is embarrassing, it's true. Donated, of
course. But how else, to work under the table? If not murder.
Morthor. It's all the same to me. No, it's much better than writing, for just one example. Scooping fish heads and ice? For
another! Didn't mind it at all, while the back was up to it.
Honest work. Fish sticks every day. Today's a different matter.
Today's a different back. And there's mercury in the fishsticks,
it's like eating breaded thermometers. And so, it's the perseverance of the organism. Despite all. Despite morality, despite
ethics, driven entirely by the price of Bombay Sapphire martinis. Life's dwindling pleasures. And the kidneys? The diabetes?
The cancers? All in good time. Which came first, the cancer or

the martini? All depends on how much of a start you give them, the one or the other. Jump in. Here comes Upside. Christ. I don't give a shit, says Upside peremptorily. You never did, says the smart money. Put a hinge on it, swing it up your ass, replies Upside. That's not a positive attitude, you point out. At least I don't go round killin' people, Upside retorts. Oho! the smart money says, a regrettable glimmer of sentience. What? He's just saying that. Can't be too careful. Come on, you ask, how in the hell am I going to get paid to kill this guy? No way, confirms the smart money, although you might be able to take up a collection. What's the minimum, you think. Donation? Collection? Smart money shrugs. Fifty bucks, you say. And when you're through fuckin' yourself in the ass, Upside starts in. Quiet, the smart money says, we're discussing your fate. Is it true love, in the ass? you quote aloud. It's narcissism, Upside insists. Or loneliness, you mention. You're never alone when you're a schizophrenic, Upside points out pointedly. How did we get onto this subject, the smart money bristles. Which subject, asshole? Upside bridles, I'm ready for all of 'em. He got between us and the bar, you point out. Upside isn't between us and the bar, the smart money points out, your pecuniary decrepitude is. Maybe it's a charity bar, you suggest lamely. Yeah, Upside roars, and the rest of the whole world is a charity whorehouse. Which just goes to show, the smart money points out, nobody is doing anything for free. Writing, least of all, you point out. How does writing keep getting into this? the smart money demands testily. You don't know anything about writing, all you know about is scooping fishheads and ice. So long as its under the table, you point out. Is it true writing, under the table? That's a good question, Upside replies, blowing smoke into my face. Why don't you get down there and find out? No table, no writing, the smart money bemoans. Can we get back on the subject of what

we're going to eat, I insist, thence onto that of how we're going
to get enough money to drink? No flag, the smart money notes.
I'm sorry I brought it up, you finally articulate. If you had a
computer, you could Google your employment. Get their picture, their location, their habits. Yeah but, the smart money
says, then they could trace you by your IP address. Not good,
you agree. Right there on the bridge abutment, the smart
money points out, and you don't even have to turn around to
see the numbers, blazed across the parapet in light-emitting
diodes: 192.334.3.101, with subnet mask and router address. I
never did figure out what a IPv6 Address is, says Upside sadly.
Your only hope would be that the advertisers would offer more
money for the information than the police. Safe at last, Upside
grins. It's not something you can put a hinge on, you point out
snidely. Say, reacts Upside, why don't you —. Get on your way,
the smart money suggests. Because it's true, you know. What's
true, Upside wants to know. It's true that you might find your
account discontinued. Upside turns pale. It's the first time
you've seen this. But the smart money is a genius. You've always
known it. I'll be going, then, Upside suggests. That you will, the
smart money agrees. We're in a rut, you suggest, as you watch
the bum make his way down the sidewalk, scaring the citizens,
scattering pigeons, briefly attracting one of the last of the
monarch butterflies. His odor reeks of *Lepidoptera* in rut.
Don't be disgusting, says the smart money, its his coloration.
How would you feel, if you only lived for three days? Betrayed,
came the honest response, but relieved. Pupation alone. Dot
dot dot, you declare bitterly, the three-day ellipsis. Often that's
all you can say, says the smart money. True, you reluctantly
agree. It's a mystery. Not like incunabula. Actually, the smart
money warms to his subject, an incunabulum is the first stage
of anything. And so we're back to pupation, you conclude, wryly

forlorn. Let me get this straight: Simply because Upside made a passing reference to murder for hire, you're going to kill him? Do you have a better suggestion? Sure. Let them arrest you, put you in jail, take their time gathering evidence, bring you to trial, convict you, and send you to Florence, Colorado, for the rest of your life, where, at least, you'll get to have a daily discussion of the ins and outs of the human being as a herd animal with Theodore Kaczynski, a.k.a. the Unabomber.

The best place, to me, was the largest remnant of this plateau that dates from the tertiary age. It's kind of rolling country, not flat, and when you get to the edge of it you find these ravines that cut very steeply into cliff-like drop-offs and there was even a waterfall there. It was a two days hike from my cabin. That was the best spot until the summer of 1983. That summer there were too many people around my cabin so I decided I needed some peace. I went back to the plateau and when I got there I found they had put a road right through the middle of it...You just can't imagine how upset I was. It was from that point on I decided that, rather than trying to acquire further wilderness skills, I would work on getting back at the system. Revenge.

You've got it memorized, you marvel. Just imagine, says the smart money, hearing that from the horse's mouth. Any horse's mouth, you agree. Kaczynski knows the work of Jacques Ellul, too. Who's that. "Organized sports pave the road to fascism." That guy? Guilt by association. It's cold there, too, in winter. Where? Florence, Colorado. Not to mention, maybe Mr. Kaczynski has better things to do than to discuss philosophy with a mere...What is it you are, anyway. Who are you, exactly? Whence come you? Whither goest? Hither, ghost. A man who likes a martini, now and again and, knowing that, all the rest is to-ing, fro-ing, and planetary pass-pass. Yes. Well, maybe we should terminate the jerkoff. So we may continue? Nobody will miss him. Except you. And how does that work. You both thrive on adversarial encounters. In other words, it's exactly like work. In other words, you'll miss each other. But, in so many words, how can you miss me when I've blown you away. You are taking the trouble to raise mighty paradigms of consciousness, when all you seek are efficacious paragons of oblivion. A.k.a. Martini-ville. So long as your liver, kidneys and metabolism hold out. For god's sakes, they've lasted this long…Snap. You didn't. His back was turned. You can't just…I did just. You didn't even take up a collection. That'll spread the blame evenly, until it covers the level places one molecule thick, a wax indiscernible. When's the last time you talked to a cop. The last time one talked to me. And the charge was…? Jaywalking in filth. Pretty serious. To the manner born. That's manor. Away from the manor borne. In a litter, one suspects. In filthy litter. And is it true love, in filthy litter? Another excellent question. Can't you just feel it, when you've run out your string? Oh, yes. Is it not a queasy sensation? It is indeed. Fear inducing? You wouldn't go that far. How far would you go? Just as goddamn far as I can. It's the human instinct. Animals, too. With or without Jesus? Does Jesus want to come along? Some would say he already came along, and then some. Some say almost anything. We were talking about string. Yes, string. Or twine. Made from recycled incunabula. String in pupation. That was a long time ago, butterfly. You've had your fun. Ah yes, fun. How long do you think this can go on, under the bridge? As long as they don't get television, under the bridge. Then what? Then out in a blaze of counterintuitive behavior. But on a day like today? I'm with Upside, on a day like today. I thought Upside was sleeping with the angels. Hah. Hey angel, put a hinge on it. That's him. See? You miss him already. Actually, you didn't miss him until his name came up. It's the ravine without the road down the middle of it that I miss. Listen, my friend. What's that? If you were to find yourself in the midst of that ravine without the road down the middle of it, you'd quickly starve or freeze to death, or find yourself consumed by some large animal, an alternative to your cheesy drama of alcohol deprivation. Precisely. My protein would serve a higher purpose. Without a doubt. One entertains not a glimmer of doubt, not a gleam, that you could do some carnivore a world of good, the very contrapositive of the proposition that you're doing nobody, not even yourself, no good whatsoever as mere entity assaying itself, pillar to post, in a feckless haze of alcohol deprivation. A travesty of humanity. Precisely. And what about that woman to whom I returned her dropped purse? Must you insist? A cop was watching from across the street. You admit it was brilliant. And if she hadn't proffered you a twenty? I might have clocked her. Despite the police officer? To spite the police officer. That makes you the very brother of Upside. A man of commodious jacket. It's true, his record is yards long, a veritable Golgolian overcoat. Was. Was. And there's the rub. How to make myth of misery? Like Gogol. Not precisely. You were speaking personally. That's true. Your personal myth. Again, I say. And what's to mythologize? You're the envy of the first world, with your independence. My independence would frighten most, and terrify others. Except Upside. If he weren't so frightened, perhaps he'd behave. How to calm him? We already took care of that. If only the small cottage, in which to be comforted by warmth, a little stove, a nine-inch television. Make it twelve. You get the point. I'd blow out my brains. I'm a son of a bitch. At last, we've nothing to argue. No, no—that twenty! What about it. It's here, in the pocket. How did you know. Numismatic anthropology. It's barely marked by filth. Perhaps it was fresh from her Automatic Teller Machine. At any rate, now all we need is a bar with extremely inexpensive vodka, ice, olives. We perhaps might dispense with martininess, which is, after all, but an affectation. For you, and you draw yourself up to your full altitude above the gutter, it is a way of life. For twenty dollars you could consume vodka on the rocks, with perhaps even a twist, for the better part of a forenoon. You don't say. You do say. Lead the way. And voilà, it wasn't a hundred yards. A lot of televisions, though. Yes, but the sound is mostly down. Yes, but it's entirely sport. Sport paves the way to multiple televisions. So it would seem. Vodka from the well and on the rocks, my good fellow. Look at that, he handed it to you at arm's length. Must have lost track of his tongs. Trade is trade, you always say. And that is some serious rotgut. If you had a charcoal filter, you could make it taste like upper-case V and G Vodka of the Gods. One must sip judiciously, so as to subscribe to the woman's breast theory of martini—that is to say, straight vodka—drinking. And what is that, the smart money asks tiredly, for the smart money has heard it all. One is not enough, three is too many. Unless you're a dog, the smart money points out, in which case, even if Romulus and Remus are splitting the dugs between them, four is the answer. Arf, you reply happily. Bartender, again, if you please. Up until this point, only your leg has been showing the jactitations of a serious philosopher. The first sip of the second drink, however, and you start rocking on your stool. Somebody plays the jukebox. It's "Nesun Dorma". And the beast is soothèd, sighs the smart money. Only in San Francisco do meet the happy conjunction of Puccini and homelessness. What the hell kind of jukebox is that, you ask. It's a Heavenly Jukebox, the smart money rejoins. Where's your sense of humour. And who is singing? Beniamino Gigli. When the Caliphate reigns, you scowl, this music is going to mean nothing to nobody. You'll be a bag of bones in a culvert by then, declares the smart money. Their kitharas will fall on deaf ears. And the call to prayer? Ditto. Five times a day, I hear. So? says the smart money, show them an alternative. Something to shoot for. The bare arms of a woman? Unacceptable, apparently. Disneyland? Please. Two hundred fifty-five sports channels? The tentacles of the mind, having embraced the western hemisphere, begin to wither. Salt on a slug, you suggest. Dust to a sinus, the smart money counters. The mores of the future, you put up. Are the rays of wireless technology, the smart money replies. The IP address, you stipulate. Is the only address, the smart money castigates. The marriage of heaven and hell, you dredge desperately. Looks like Detroit, the smart money suggests. Don't distract me, you beg. Have another sip. Right after the one I just had? The very one. Two guys come in. We're down to ten bucks. They look like they can afford to be anywhere. To tip or not to tip? But they had to come in here. Not if you want a fourth drink. Cadge 'em for a drink. You don't have those kind of social skills. Tell you what. What. We get a round off one or both those guys? Yeah? We leave a tip. Now that, allowed the smart money, is transactionalism. That guy went oh for six, one guy is saying, in post-season. Who the hell cares about post-season? you jump in. Yeah, says the second guy, tell it like it is. It's pre-season that counts, you insist. They both look at you. Right? you declare, am I right? You got to get to post-season, the first guy says. That's a long way. What are you, nuts? you say. Are telling me the fucking journey is the fucking reward? you say. Some spiritual shit like that? Yeah, the second guy grins, elbowing the first guy. What are you drinking, buddy? The clear, you say. I'll have a screwdriver, the guy says, he'll have whatever pilsner you got, and let me get a glass of clear—he leans down over the bar, to look past his friend—clear what? he asks. Vodka from the well, the bartender fills in the blank tiredly. Some people just got a natural knack for curtailing humanity. What I want curtailed is defensive hitting, says the first guy, solid, defensive, hitting. I don't care how they do it. Well I—you begin. Can it, the smart money suggests. What's that, lil' buddy? the second guy says. Nothing, you mutter into your drink. I just love getting drunk in the morning. It doesn't really help that much, the first guy says. Help what, you say. The Giants, the first guy says. I thought we were talking about the 'Niners, you say. They just don't play that much better when I'm drunk. Me neither, the second guy says morosely. Me three, you say into your glass, totally at a loss. Every time you float one of these sports gambits, you say to yourself, you quickly find yourself all at sea. Sailing is a sport, the smart money observes. Is it ever, you smile dreamily, holding up your half-empty glass. Some days, life is good.

SIX

THE HEAD IS A LEGACY CODEBASE, AND YOU'RE THE ONLY PERSON getting paid to maintain it. Your head got off a troop ship from Korea at Pier 21 in 1954, you took your head into the first bar you saw on the waterfront, the first bar you'd seen in two years, you had a nice chat with the guy on the stool next to yours while the two of you ate a dynamite one-dollar lunch, and, after the guy bought you a round and left, the bartender told you the guy was Mayor Lapham. Your head got off the long-gone Fell Street off-ramp with two dollars and a dog in 1973, within two weeks you had a job, an apartment, a girl, and it's still going on like that. Your lesbian band broke up in San Francisco while on tour in 1991, it's 2004 and your housecleaning business is bringing down $300,000 year, you still don't know what you really want to do, but you like not knowing it in San Francisco. The town is full of these kinds of people. You, you could have been home-less in the Big Apple, gotten a real taste of the big time, freez-ing in abandoned train tunnels with rats the size of capybaras—the works; but no, you'd rather be homeless in San Francisco. There's just something about this city. There's a lot about this city. You get tired of being homeless, for example, I mean, every-body gets tired of who they are every once in a while, no? You get tired of being homeless? You get tired of sitting on a milk carton, leaning against the chain link fence that surrounds the

symphony musician's parking lot on Hayes between Octavia
and Gough, an otherwise excellent location you've held down
for twenty-five or thirty years, on account the rich pedestrian
traffic, and the traffic in rich pedestrians, opera swells, symphony patrons, ballet mavens, and city hall regulars, they all eat
around there, park around there, get loaded around there, and
it's not too tough to get three squares a day and enough 40 oz.
malt liquors to stay comfortable, not to mention the excellent
southern exposure, which will last until the city decides what to
do with the their vacant lot across the street. San Francisco is
an easy city to be homeless in, but—you get tired of your routine? Stash your gear under the steps of the lawyer's offices at
the corner of Ivy and Octavia, and head out. Take a bus part of
the way if you want to, after all, you qualify for the senior dis-
count, if you have the sixty cents, out Geary to Arguello, say. Jog
over to Clement Street, which is forty blocks of Asia redolent of
ginger, garlic, chicken, duck, cardamom, sage, sausage, steamed
rice, coffee houses, tea houses, bars, restaurants, grocery and
produce stores, and walk it to the Pacific. There you'll find big
swells arriving all the way from Japan smashing into rocks and
cliff faces that have somehow been putting up with it since the
end of the ice age, where they atomize heaving brine into a salty
mist, and where you can harvest miner's lettuce in the stream
that drained through the Sutro Baths one hundred years ago, or
marvel at the way sea lions can get the gnarliest swell to neatly
deposit them high up Seal Rock, just beyond Point Lobos,
where the sign says Danger: People Have Been Swept From
These Rocks And Drowned, and ne'er true words have been
incised by pity and pitted by pitilessness. In fact, if you're really tired of being homeless, you can let this happen to you. And
it's got that loneliness, too, out there. Rain or shine, wind or no,
couples holding hands or a pair of seagulls fighting over a fully

dressed hot dog, there are fewer lonelier places in the world
than Land's End, the far western edge of the civilized world,
whence you know if you journey to the next inhabited piece of
land, Hawaii, or Japan, say, or China or Australia, or various
archipelagos, say, wherever you go after this, you're going to
have to start all over, and that won't do, you're too old to start
over. And it's cold there, at Land's End. There are a coffee joint,
a hot-dog stand, a restaurant and a parking lot, and tourists,
dogs on the beach—and what a beach, it's called Ocean Beach,
and it goes for miles. And it's lonely as hell out there, lonely and
staggeringly beautiful. That's the pincers. That's the threat to
the codebase, that's the net content of the codebase. But you,
yes, you, even there, you're not alone. Being alone's overrated,
observes the smart money, as you watch a surfer get boiled.
Fifty-three degree water, and this guy manages to get boiled.
He loves it. He must. If you'd taken up surfing while your codebase was still tender and malleable, the smart money starts in,
you'd be a very happy real estate dealer by now. That seems an
inherent contradiction, you say. Wife, three kids, big house
overlooking this very beach, the smart money persists, five or
six surfboards per each surfing member of the family taking up
all the space in the garage, maybe, so everybody could surf
every morning before they take the bus to school and you drive
your electric car down to the office. Could I work from home?
you say, tentatively hopeful. For the tax write-off, the smart
money recognizes. Didn't know I was that smart, did you. In a
word, no. Besides, where might it have gotten me, if I'd been
forced to lead a normal life? I'd have ended up killing the entire
family and myself too. That maddening? *Sans doute.* Sure. Just
the hint of a television, let alone its pervasive presence, would
one day send you right over the edge. Naturally, your demesne
would be bristling with weapons because you never know when

the government is going to take away your weapons, and then they're going to come after you. And then one day, if only for a moment, you wake up to the fact that they are you, and, vice versa, you is they. Now we're talking number agreement, as expressed by singular and plural verbs and nouns. But wait, you were on to something. I'm always onto something. You is they and they are you. Oh yes. One day for some reason the television stays off just long enough for you to realize that the thing you fear most is yourself, not the outside world, but the inside world, and that, even though you live in San Francisco, your life is meaningless. It's true that a bracing immersion in the Pacific, a very stroke or two off the beach and you're fighting for your life, everything's changed, of course you want to live, you were just kidding and you have to take a deep breath, submerge beneath the rollers and the tide you'd failed to notice is ebbing to the tune of something like five knots, and drag yourself along the bottom, clawing up great fistfuls of sand and hopefully the odd rock and some well-anchored bull kelp, until your lungs are fixing to prolapse like the guts out of the mouth of that fish from Hawaii, blow inside out, so you blast to the surface gasping for breath, the surface is further up than you thought, but you make it, the air is thick with airborne foam, you get a good lung full of scud, you inhale it anyway, and while you're choking and realizing that you've just lost the five yards you'd gained toward the beach, your head, that codebase you and you only you have been spending a great deal of time maintaining, has become part of the very machine that has become the only machine, the total machine, the machine whose mission is to cultivate efficiency from all within its realm, which is everywhere, which is now and forever, and that to be inefficient is to court death, not injury, not unemployment, but death, abrupt and final, and that some anachronism of sentiment, of some burp in finality, is the only thing between the living death you have managed to assay for yourself and the sleep of eternity. Just listen to the television: *The press secretary announced today that the President has ordered his staff to undertake a strict review of all options as regards the terrorist threat. The situation is perceived as cautiously calm, or orange. If you see the color orange, however, walk, do not run, to the nearest 911 haven. Do not worry about your spelling. Despite everything, try not to be late for work. If you are late for work, however, carry your group number with you at all times. We're going to give shut-ins, crippled people, people with special needs, and the elderly an extra month to sign up for digital television. Remember, this is not an option, it is a necessity. Congress has voted an allowance for special income collectives. While commercials are changing the outer landscape, while the human body was the romantic landscape of the twentieth century, the little screen located in the blind spot on the left lens of your sunglasses has become the romantic landscape of the twenty-first century, and if the various big internet companies don't start buying up newspapers, the internet will become a sewer, and the government will be able to do anything it wants.* The television didn't really say that— did it? Not all of it. Some of it's too obvious to restate, and therefore progressive. Why don't we just get this job over with? I'll bet they got a terrific martini up there in the Cliff House. What am I supposed to do, just wade out there and pop the guy? I don't know. Get creative. It's cold out here. That part about the television is making me sick. Everything about television makes you sick. No no, the part about it and radio and the internet seamlessly blending into a fishless sewage. Fish being the metaphor for verifiable information? That would be correct. There's a lot to fear, once you start thinking about this shit. That's the operative term. Fear? Shit. Misoscaticism. Misocatechism was bad enough. Much as the Catholic Church used to get those kids young, and I mean young, so they could bend their little minds to the Pope's will, the same shape as the Pope's nose, so, equally, mass media, which include the internet of course, can be used to twist the awareness of the general public. Soon, public opinion, as shaped by whomever has the biggest megaphone, or the busiest thumbs, or the loudest mouth, will become just that, opinion, with not a fact to trouble it, for the simple reason that the facts will not be available. Here he comes. This is rather a public place to be killing people, don't you think? Yes, I would, but it's our luck that he surfed till dark, and conditions are too rough for all but the most hardy, it's a Tuesday, everybody else has a so-called real job to be real for, this guy's self-employed or something, got it all going on, wife, three kids, big house overlooking his favorite surf break, which just happens to be in his favorite city, and oh no, here comes his goddamn wife. Who could plan these things? So the question is, do you want to kill somebody for free today? It's been a long time since you killed somebody for free. She's messing up a perfectly good plan. Did the brief say anything about a time frame? Not that you can recall; but, on the other hand, you're thirsty. She's got a towel. Does she know she's messing with his private space? That he likes being wet and cold and alone two or three days out of the week? Of course she knows it. But she has a feeling. What feeling is that. That you're out here somewhere. Somewhere? I'm right here. Ready to snap her husband. That's right. Primed, you might say. Feeling those—how many was it? One thousand, if you get them for five bucks apiece and don't leave a tip. One thousand martinis, that's right. Although you always leave a tip. Okay, and you tip generously. Do the math. It's not math, it's arith-

metic. Say you tip at the rate of twenty percent. Fair enough.
So gamma martini dollars plus point two gamma tip dollars
equals a total of five grand. Manipulate some figures, your tip
budget is $866.33. That much. So what you're really spending
on actual martinis is five thousand less $866.33 equals
$4166.67. Are you following me? No. I'm following that young
woman with the towel. That's right, keep your eye on the ball
while I parse the strategy, which is as much as to say you are
applying all the art and science at your disposal in order to
bring maximum efficiency to your decision. That's always the
case. Right. $4166.67 divided by five dollars per martini is
833.33 martinis. So few? The smart money shrugs as only the
smart money can shrug. You don't like it, drink where the martinis cost ten dollars. Okay okay, eight thirty-three point thirty-
three. Rounding down, eight hundred and thirty-three martinis. Okay okay, you sullenly agree. At five martinis per night
that makes for something like twenty-three point eight weeks
of uninterrupted blind drunkenness. Round up. Okay, twenty-
four weeks. I'm amazed we haven't done this calculation
before. We have done it before. He sees her. Winsome lass.
And three kids at home. First marriage? That information is
not available. But at the rate of five martinis per night, you're
looking at one hundred and sixty-six point six days between
jobs. Round up. Sure, one sixty-seven—that's if you spend the
money on nothing but martinis. An SRO hotel in this town is
four hundred a week. Sooner of later you have to deal with
food, and food costs something. Say another hundred a week
for food. Make it seventy-five, I been putting on weight. Okay,
one month, that's four times one hundred seventy-five—. Wait,
I can do it easier: two seventy-fives is one-fifty times two
makes three hundred, plus four weeks at four hundred makes
sixteen—nineteen hundred a month for roof and rashers. Back

nineteen hundred out of the five thousand. Thirty-one hundred. Correct. Recrank your all-purpose equation. Uh, I might have to scratch that one out in the sand. Help yourself, the tide is out, you got six hours. Gamma dollars plus point two zero gamma dollars equals three one zero zero dollars. Collect terms. One point two times gamma equals three one zero zero. Manipulate. Gamma equals three one oh oh divided by one point two. Move the decimal to the right in the divisor, add a zero to the dividend. Twelve into thirty-one goes twice, two times twelve makes twenty-four, subtract, seventy, twelve into seventy goes six no five times, sixty, subtract, ten, drop down a zero, one hundred, ah, ah, twelve goes into one hundred eight times, which gives ninety-six, subtract, twelve goes into forty thrice, point thrice, three times twelve makes thirty-six, subtract, another forty, another three, another thirty-six, ad infinitum. Twenty-five hundred eighty-three point three three three. Dollars. Subtract that from the thirty-one hundred— five hundred sixteen point sixty-seven tip dollars. Now divide that upper figure by five. Five dollars per martini? That would be the presumption. Okay. Five into twenty-five would be five, times five makes twenty-five again, subtract, zero, bring down the eight, divide by five equals one, times five makes five, subtracting yields three, too small for the five gives a cold forefinger and an aching back bring down the three, bring down the three, my mind is locking up, keep going, it's getting dark, perseverance furthers, thirty-three, five into thirty-three makes six, times five is thirty, subtract, three, too small, bring down the next three, fives into thirty-threes yield sixes ad infinitum, round up to seven, and thence up to seven again, to the left of the decimal, nice, five hundred seventeen martinis and not a dime left over. Divide by five martinis per night, yeah, and voilà, one hundred and three point four nights. Well over three months. Now what you got to do, ideally, is establish an expression that will precisely match the amount of time you can afford to stay in an SRO hotel with the exact number of martinis you can swill and still have a place to crash. Let's call gamma—hey. Gamma…Hey! What the—? HEY!! Who the—. You're stepping on my calculations! Get the fuck off my calculations, motherfucker! Yes you! And her! Get her off! No, this is my part of the beach. You? You? You? You got the whole goddamn ocean to fuck around in. Go ah way! Away! See all that work—this, I'm dragging my foot around your mess— this was the culmination of all those figures. Those! These! Son of a bitch! The guy just broke his board over my head! The nerve! All he and his stupid wife had to do was walk around these calculations and everything would have been fine. He didn't have to die today. He could have died tomorrow—and his wife would have been saved! She could have raised the children in his memory! But no. No! The guy has to ask, he has to invite— no, he practically has to beg me to re-arbitrate his goddamn fate. Maybe he really is sick of watching television. Maybe she really did intrude upon his little bit of private space, in which he communes with mother ocean. Maybe his is a bad mood and he really feels like laying off some of the action onto this ostensible hapless ostensible homeless ostensible guy on his beach, the only other person that's out here in this blistering cold and now that the fog is in completely dark night. My figures. All that work. So now they both had to die. That's all there was to it. It's a done deal. Get paid, get one free. More orphans in the world. Like I give a fuck. We'll wing that bit about the martinis. We'll find out how many martinis there are to be had for five grand in a world that expects twenty percent tips for tending bar and four hundred dollars a week for flea-raddled SRO hotels and seventy-five a week for a can of soup per day and one of those snack packs with twelve orange crackers and six slices each of baloney and white cheese, although one prefers the yellow cheese and olive loaf but those are harder to find and more expensive when you do find them...What a world. What a world. What a world...

SEVEN

SOMETIMES, LYING IN MY NEST AND LISTENING TO BENIAMINO Gigli on somebody's orphaned earbuds, I think that it may just be the perfect way go out. You discern with precision. I've got the massive overdose of oxycodone, stashed in one of the hollow tubes of my Denali Summit tent. Don't forget, by the way, that much in the way that lame is an anagram of male, Denali is an anagram of Denial. I figure I could wash it down with a third martini and maybe make it back to the nest from the bar before the inner sun sets. While I genuflect towards the woman's breast theory of martini drinking, wouldn't it seem obvious that on the last day, on that day of all days, I get to have a third martini? Guys like you, the smart money says, can always come up with some excuse to make any old day special. You say, perhaps even taking out one or another of the earbuds to make your point, I got a good daydream going here, you fuck. Good daydream? the smart money cracks back, it's like you got a mini-disk playing in your mouth. No, on the contrary, I'm telling you, if you leave me alone, I can get through on my own cerebral dime and for maybe an hour the rest of the world will be safe from egregious depredation. Why don't you make like Cannonball Adderly, the smart money suggests, and for maybe the rest of your life the world will be better off, and beyond. You know, I declare, you can maybe make the case that some psychopaths are beneficent, but that just means you've never encountered the genuine article. Have you ever considered, I continued, before the smart money could interject, the fact that I have managed to channel my alienation, by way of getting paid for it, I am in fact a superior citizen? Remunerated moral turpitude makes you a superior citizen? I think not. I, on the other hand, think so. You need to reconsider. You need to back off, you're messing with my daydream. The reek of the acreage of filth in the general vicinity of your unwashed ass cheeks messes with everybody else's daydream. How can I put up with this? This, my own super-ego accusing me of anti-hygienic turpitude. If I were indeed your superego, that's what I would be here for. But, quite the contrary. Alas. The contrary indeed. You're here to make sure I don't get caught, or chastised, or penalized, to insure that my disguise remains efficacious. But, do you not see that your disguise has become yourself? Of...of course I see that. Careful. Uncertainty, like hesitation, is death. And...vice versa. The self has become the disguise. I have pared my needs to sleep, warmth, some external discomfort due to weather, what vodka or gin I can legitimately buy, the odd stint of employment, an occasional fit of rage, channeled at best, highly destructive at worst...What else? When the fit threatens, I walk to the Pacific and gaze. That's not what happened the last time. No gazing. None. Introspection, maybe, but that came later, after many martinis. These days, in fact, that's the only access I have to introspection. All else is speculation. Well, but, that was a job. Are you sure it was a job? Sure I —. If so, where is the money? The money...Why, it's spent. Spent on a drunken spree, just like always. Are you sure? Of course I'm...Well, no I'm...Now that you mention it. Now that you bring it up...When's the last time we went to Union Square? Why, three days after the beach—no? And when was the beach? Three days before we last went to Union Square. You're talking in circles. Well, the next stop after that is concentricity. Oh, how I yearn for concentricity, as I conceive of it, the very meeting place at the center, where all this restlessness will surcease. It's rumored, it's spoken of, in certain texts, religious texts. Though not in others. In others there are hints of... results, karma, karma is action, deed, event—nothing more. The mind does not know wherefore. One sleeps in a nest under a bridge, a freeway overpass, really, hard by the police station, for security, and not far from the Office of Social Security for convenience, one kills people for money, money paid under the table, one gets by. Who is to say, other than these sacred texts, whether or not that the present pathetic existence is the result of a previous pathetic existence. Shouldn't that be previously pathetic existence? In any case, how could they know? Why would they care? Well, they want to skate on the contingencies of their own pathetic previous existences. Clearly. Why else would they assay such a difficult topic, if not for self-interest. Well, since other people are interested in the results of their investigations, it might be called enlightened self-interest. And isn't that a neat trick. The next step would be to get them to pay for your investigations, that is to say, vendible self-interest. And voilà, you've got your church. Each to his own. I can't go there, I can't attend, and, since I have no money, they don't want me. But there are organizations, individuals, who would take you under their wing on account they perceive it as their duty to mankind. Helping one another. Ah, there was a woman once. Despite which, you didn't come to this pass as a misogynist. Nor, for that matter, a mystery writer. Excellent point. But what is this, if not a mystery? Where's the mystery? She arrived, she sniffed, she departed. Ah so, first act, second act, third act. I'd forgotten. Shakespeare incapsulate. It was a very long time ago.

If, in the interim, there'd been any design changes…You'd be the last person to inquire of them, or to inquire about them. Got me covered. My *modus operandi*. No, you're m.o. is arctic martinis, built with vodka drawn from the Well of Doom. I don't see that it's working, particularly. That's the problem with this outdoor life, it's good for you, salubrious, one might say, much in the way that, say, *huevos nopalitos* might be good for you, were it not for the cholesterol. Better, in other words, than eating? I wouldn't go so far as to say that. You know…It's inevitable that you get caught. Why do you speak of that now? Here? Today? That's a cop over there. Two of them. How can you tell? It's the flannel shirts, the sensible shoes, the jeans, the nylon jackets, the identical moustaches, the pasty complexions and a certain heaviness about the jowls. I think you have something there. Let us hale them. Better we should wait for them to hale us. Good morning officers. Officers, says the one, looking to the other, his companion, who does not take his eye off of us. Now why would you draw such a conclusion as that? It's the shirts, the jackets, the bulge in the small of the back, under the nylon jacket, the bags under all four of your eyes, the unkempt state of the two moustaches, the near-constant anxiety about the 'Niners—you need more? The two of them consider you for a moment. Then one of them shows you a photograph. Don't touch it, he says, pulling it back, just look at it. Remain downwind, please. While a bad photograph, it's sufficiently detailed to reveal a smiling young couple, she embracing him from behind, her chin on his shoulder, the two of them absolutely trusting the possibility of the image the camera might give back to them. A handsome brace of Caucasians, you allow, clapping a lid on your hostility. Do I know them? Do you? asks one of the officers. I do not, you reply. Should I? Do you know I know them? It's not for lack of confusion, you gesture to either side, that I find myself in my present circumstances. We have no idea whether or not you knew them, the officer says, turning the photograph so that he himself might have a look at the young couple. Could you speak up, I ask him. The traffic doesn't interfere much with my stream of consciousness, but it does hamper ordinary communication. So you don't know them, he shows the photograph again. Don't touch it. I withdraw my filthy claw. Not that I recall. Never seen them. Not that I recall. What's your name? Not that I recall. Come again? Not that I recall. We need to see some identification. Please. There's the Social Security paperwork, of course. But I don't drive or have an address. So you must once have been a dues-paying member of society, an officer says. What is this, you gesture left and right, if not society. How's that. He shows me my own card. In order to be eligible. It must be true, I tell him. What did you do? Before she left me, you suddenly blurt, I wired missiles for that big Air Force contractor, down to Cupertino. Wired missiles, the guy says, incredulous. It was morally repugnant, you advise him. Not like being a cop. Where is this going? his partner says. Take it easy, the first cop says. That's a nasty bruise on your head, he says. Once a week, you gesture left and right, I get beat up out here. Everybody does. Did you report it? You laugh in his face. These people are dead, the first cop tells him. What am I, a potted plant? his partner snaps. Yeah, you say, to no good purpose. You stay out of this, the first cop tells you. You shake your head. The very movement gives them a taste of your effluvium. Wasn't this interview your idea? you ask him. I believe it was, his partner says, looking at him, not you. My card, I remind him, extending a filthy claw. Pinching its corner between thumb and forefinger, he dangles it above my palm. I grasp it. Social Security doesn't pay you enough to get your own place, huh, he says, not unkindly. I drinks a bit, I tell him with a shrug, and you need a fixed address. Do the math. Somebody subtracted this nice couple from the world's equation, the first cop says. His partner winces. You just look at him. After a while, he blinks. How can you live like this, he abruptly expostulates. I haven't heard that question in a long time, you say to him, not without tenderness, how kind. Do you know the poem? If he'd been bitten by a bullet ant, the guy could not have started more violently. No, his partner says with a charmed smile. Let's have it. Left fist on left hip, with the right hand somewhat aloft, you let them have it.

> The world is too much with us; late and soon,
> Getting and spending, we lay waste our powers;
> Little we see in Nature that is ours;
> We have given our hearts away, a sordid boon!
> This Sea that bares her bosom to the moon,
> The winds that will be howling at all hours,
> And are up-gathered now like sleeping flowers,
> For this, for everything, we are out of tune;
> It moves us not. —Great God! I'd rather be
> A Pagan suckled in a creed outworn;
> So might I, standing on this pleasant lea,
> Have glimpses that would make me less forlorn;
> Have sight of Proteus rising from the sea;
> Or hear old Triton blow his wreathèd horn.

The sound of traffic over our heads and at right angles to that of the street below, seemed momentarily to have dimmed. For once you can actually hear the hundreds of plastic bags, trapped in the concertina wire atop the chain link fence, as they rattle in the westerly. If you were sufficiently paranoid, the graffiti on the abutment might have ceased their wriggling. But your back is turned. Both cops sigh loudly, each in his own way. Try reciting that, next time you're drunk along the parapet below the Cliff House on a stormy night, the smart money suggests to them, for the which, in a private aside, he congratulates me on having completely derailed the conversation. Wordsworth, the second cop says softly. I think that's Wordsworth. Think? you respond. The fuzzicle knows! Fuzzicle, the second cop smiles. I haven't heard that in a long time. The term or the poem. Both. What's it mean, his partner, who is considerably younger, more earnest, less jaded, harder, and maybe stupider than the second cop, asks, narrowing his eyes. The term or the poem. The term. It's hard to translate, the second cop, pocketing the photograph, tells him. So is the poem, I guess. If you can't hear the music, I can't explain it to you, he adds, as Louis Armstrong once said. Certain neighborhoods in this town, I confide to his partner, they're only to happy to lick fuzzicles. The implication was, of course, that maybe they might want to take a trip to one of those neighborhoods. It's a lot tougher around here, I gesture at our surroundings. Here we educate them. A truck with a loose roll-up door on the back of its enclosed bed slams and bangs its way under the overpass. To me it sounds like crockery swimming upstream against my tinnitus. To the cops it sounds like gunfire, and they duck while reaching for their weapons. Whoa, whoa, you say. Take it easy, fellas. Four, the friendlier one explains as he straightens up, count them, four cops got shot in Oakland last week. Dead? you inquire tentatively. He nods. And I can see that his partner is wrapped about as tight as it's possible to be wrapped while remaining on his side of the invisible fence that stands between us. On his side of the badge, in so many words. I'm sorry to hear that, I say truthfully, for, truthfully, there are some real motherfuckers out there, some of them with automatic weapons, which thought the smart money congratulates me for having the presence of mind to pronounce out loud. It's the upper-case G God's truth, the second cop says to me. But what's it have to do with this asshole, his partner interjects, clearly drained of patience. This guys is not an asshole, his elder corrects him, he is a citizen until proved otherwise. How about them 'Niners, I brazenly query. The younger guy raises an eyebrow. I thought everything was okay until they passed on renewing Sybley's contract, he says in all sincerity. I can see you know how to mix with the hoi polloi, I tell him. Or maybe it was the smart money tells him that. This is the most sustained conversation I've had with another human being since I applied for Social Security, two years ago, or was it one, I'm beginning to lose track. And then they fucked up on their first three draft picks, the younger cop continues. His partner, however, is watching me. So they've practiced this routine, and maybe they're not so far out of their depth as they want to appear to be wading. But it's them on my territory, at the moment, and not the other way around. They'll never regain the glory of the seventies, you tell the guy kindly, but with certainty. Or was it the eighties, I'm beginning to lose track. I wasn't around for that, the younger cop says, narrowing his mouth, I'm tired of hearing about it from you old guys, I want a piece of the glory, like, now. It's all about building, the smart money says to him, somewhat paternally, and his partner agrees. Takes time, he says to the kid, to build up the bench, get the drills regular, to lock in conditioning, to gel the team, to find the magic. You know? Yeah, I jump in. The magic. They're taking they're sweet time about it, the kid grouses, and I'm getting old waiting for them to find it. Old? His partner and I both get a laugh out of this. Damn, observes the smart money, you haven't laughed out loud in a long time. Say, you say aloud, until you guys showed up, things out here have been slower than sub-zero suppuration. You should come around more often. Most of the other people out here, you gesture right, you gesture left, only want to talk about scatological homologues. Most of the time, anyway. Scatology can be most poetic, the second, older cop points out. Are we still talking about the 'Niners, the first cop asks suspiciously. Because if we aren't we need to be getting on with this. There comes a pause while these two now both watch me expectantly. I shake my head, puzzled. And what, exactly, I ask, is 'this'? It's a criminal investigation, the kid jumps in. This couple, he indicated the breast of his partner's shirt, wherein by then resided the aforementioned photograph, got themselves most cruelly terminated at Land's End last night. The only witness we can find says he saw a homeless person very near to the scene. He looks at you. No, says the smart money, he's looking at you. Then he's looking into a black hole. And that just about narrows it down, doesn't it, I tell the cops. It does, actually, the older of them replies cheerfully. There's only a little over six thousand of you. He shrugs. And you're not all that hard to find. Six thousand? you say. And you're going to talk to all of us? Just the men, the younger one says, a little over half of you. Fifty-two percent, his partner puts in. Three thousand three hundred and sixteen adult males. The rest are women and kids, the younger cop clarifies. You're talking my language, the smart money tells him. He frowns slightly. How's that? I just love arithmetic, he gets to hear. I'm sighing deeply, if inwardly, I tell the smart money, *sotto voce* of course. I prefer poetry, the older cop gets to say. I repeat, I repeat, you're going to talk to all of them? All of them, the younger cop says, if that's what it takes. But we'll probably narrow it down considerably before then. Good luck, I say. You want a card, so you can call us if you hear anything? No phone, I offer lamely. I thought all you people out here had phones, the old one says, these days. Where'd you hear that? I ask him. Just observation, he replies. But sure, I say, cozening up to the obvious, give me a card. You never know, says the older cop, dealing me a calling card, from a deck of them secured with a rubber band, its corner pinched between his thumb and forefinger. Yeah, I say, taking its opposite corner likewise, as a matter of courtesy and perhaps hygiene. You never know.

EIGHT

I'LL BET THAT'S THE GUY, YOU OVERHEARD THE ELDER COP SAY TO the younger one over the roof of their unmarked cruiser, which was parked at the foot of the berm that sloped up to the bridge abutment. The younger one paused. How can you tell. He's listening to us. Oh? The younger one turned for a look in my direction. And, though they were barely discernible over the roar of traffic overhead, you were listening to them. And you're still listening to them. Huh, said the younger one, as he slid behind the wheel. So what are going to—and he slammed the door. The older one, very casual, gave the appearance of not caring one way or another. He tapped his phone on the roof of the car as if he had his own, very faraway thoughts, then himself slipped into the passenger seat. The engine started, though I couldn't hear it. Your ass is fixin' to be in a sling, the smart money said, as the car moved into traffic, rounded the corner, beyond the onramp, and disappeared. My ass? What about your ass? They got nothing on me, the smart money said. They don't even know I exist. I suppose we should get rid of the weapon. You should get rid of the weapon, and I know just the guy. Who's that? Riparian Sam, the smart money said. I had to think about that one. But then—you mean the guy who approached us about purchasing a weapon, awhile back?

The very same. But where is he? And how can I just hand off our piece to the guy? Our piece. We hand off your piece. Yeah yeah. But how? You sell it to him, dummy. He's the one offering to buy. Tell him you happened to come across the merchandise, make a deal, go your separate ways, dime him to the cops—you got the card—. It's true, I'm fingering the calling card among the filth in my pocket, I've got the card. —and get drunk on the proceeds, the smart money concluded, confident that the red herring has been dragged across the bloodhound's trail. And so it went. Riparian Sam liked to spend his days sitting at a picnic bench under a stunted Monterey pine hard by a public fishing pier, a bit of green along Terry A. Francois Boulevard called, imaginatively enough, Agua Vista Park. And that's what he did there, he stared at the water. One day six or seven years ago, a guy sat down opposite him, interrupting Sam's view of the water, and wouldn't get up again. They got into a fight, Riparian Sam got the worst of it, and ever since then he'd been talking about getting hold of a gun and killing the guy. Six or seven years. He sat at that bench all day and, just as long as you didn't install yourself between him and his view of the water, he'd talk to you about getting a gun and killing the last guy who had done so. As you might imagine, as a rule, day in and day out, Riparian Sam had the Agua Vista pretty much to himself. So the smart money and I put the gun into the middle of a bunch of trash in a shopping cart and pushed it down all the way down Fifth Street to Bluxome, east two blocks to Fourth Street, right on Fourth and past the train station and over the Mission Creek drawbridge and across Third Street onto Mission Rock St., thence it's but a hundred yards to the north end of Terry Francois Boulevard, and past the Bay View Boat Club and its boat ramp and along the western bank of the San Francisco Bay to Agua Vista Park where, no surprise whatsoever, Riparian Sam sat with his back to the afternoon sun and his face, brown as the girth strap on a forest service jackass, turned east toward the bay and Oakland. Sam, the smart money opens up, how the fug are ya. I'm lookin to kill me an interloper, Sam starts right in. Just need to find me a pistol so I can git on with it. Well I got just the feller here for ya. The smart money gives me a nudge. Ah, yes, ahem, I blunder in, and just what caliber of weapon might you seek? Big bore, Riparian says without hesitation. Though he does not make eye contact with you, you can practically see the cranes of the container port, six miles across the bay, reflected in his eyes. Don't fuckin sit there, he adds severely. It's like a pitbull tied to a fence on a short chain, the smart money observes, you want to get only so close. Would a twenty-five do? you ask him as if timidly. Goddamn woman's gun, Sam says without hesitation. Oh? Well, you reply, I've found it to be ideally suited. How's that? Sam asks unexpectedly. Unexpectedly, because you'd expect a guy like Riparian Sam, a man of many fixed opinions, to not countenance a contradiction to one of them. Well, you say, warming to the subject, it doesn't make much noise, it shoots straight, rounds aren't all that hard to come by, once you leave the city, although I can help you out with that if you're short on transportation, they're centerfire, just in case you're a handloader, and you look the type to me, a perfectionist, interested in all things, and—. I'll just be using the one round, Sam declares flatly. Just the one round, you repeat. Just the one, he repeats. One round, one bastard. He moved his chin. Sat right there, he did. Did he, you parrot. Wouldn't move the whole day, Sam continued, his back to me and not so much as a please and thankyou. Rude, you allow. Needs taught some manners, Sam agreed. Seen him lately? the smart money thinks to ask. Sam's brow furrows. Can't recall, he says after a while. Probably not, the smart money concludes. Oh, he's around, Sam predicted. And I'll find him. Does that mean you're going to leave your spot? I asked. Riparian Sam thought about this. All I'd really have to do, he said, assuming a cagey look, would be to sit here and wait for him. When he shows, I don't even give him a tumble, see. He sits right there. He raised his finger and pointed. Right in front of me, right between me and the Oakland International Container Terminal. I thought that's what he was looking at, the smart money says, with a glance across the blue water. Let him get settled in, Riparian Sam says. And now his thumb stands up, at right angles to his fore-finger. Let him get comfortable. The thumb extends back, away from the forefinger, as far as it can be made to go. Pow, Sam said. The finger recoiled. More like snap, you think to correct him, but you let it go. Drill 'em right dang dab in the occiput. Say, Sam blinks, do ya think a thirty-two would blow his two or three brains as far as that pier? The pistol is a .25, the pier is twenty yards away. The smart money looks at it and makes a calculation. Only if you hold the piece at arm's length, the smart money says. But don't touch the muzzle to the back of his head, it might give you away. Oh. Riparian Sam lowers the shooting finger and its hand to the plastic 2x8 that makes up his edge of the picnic table. How much, he asks after a while. How much you got, you ask him. Check came last week, Sam muses. Weather's nice, the smart money says. Been sleeping out? Not in, Sam says. Out, then, you conclude. Give me fifty bucks. A shadow passes over Riparian Sam's face, like that of a cloud over a freshly manured field in the heart of the Imperial Valley. That's funny, Sam says. How that? you ask. It just so happens I got fifty bucks, he says. Got change for a twenty? Absolutely not, the smart money says. I'll give you sixty, then, Sam says. He speaks in a monotone. Revenge is worth whatever it costs to pay for it, you adduce. You sound like Orestes, the smart money says. I could use a little rest, Sam says. But duty calls. In consideration of the ten bucks we—I—will thrown in an extra clip with rounds, you say. Only need the one slug, Sam says. Come on, Sam, you say, a deal's a deal. Keep your goddamn extra clip and rounds, Sam snarls. You going to follow through on this deal or not? Are you going to go back on your word? He turns his head, and his gaze could not have remained more level if it had been the ruby beam of a laser theodolite. Am I gonna have to add you to the list? he asks. Huh? If so, let me have two rounds. Or, he leans forward and stares directly into your eyes, is this job gonna require *three* rounds? His breath reeks of fortified grape distillate. Like yours, the smart money says. No wonder his lip is quivering, you conclude. No, the smart money says. No, you repeat, you needn't. But please accept what rounds remain in the existing clip, and please don't discharge it until you can no longer hear the practically-disintegrated bearings in the rapidly departing wheels of this shopping cart. Done, Riparian agrees, resuming his regal stare out over the bay. There's nobody around, a matter of privacy and personal space that Sam's been seeing to for years—ever since the city built this park, it's said. So you hand him the pistol, neatly disguised as a dozen eggs. It's an automatic, you begin to explain. But Riparian Sam already has the piece out of the egg carton and is turning it this way and that and quite expertly, you notice. Another fucking Gulf War vet, the smart money grumbles. That's the safety, you begin to explain anyway. But then Sam clicks off the safety with disconcerting familiarity, as if he's owned this particular pistol all his life, and been shooting it too, which only reinforces the impression to be gained when he sticks the business end of it right in your face. Let's see, Sam says. And rotates the extended arm ninety degrees and snaps off a round. A two-inch splinter twirls off the farthest piling of the fishing pier, perhaps forty yards downrange, and, though no louder than the crack of a bullwhip, the discharge slaps across the water. Jeeze, you tell him, involuntarily looking around, discharging a firearm within city limits is a big-time felony. Nice piece, Riparian Sam says, holding the pistol up for inspection. Shoots straight. He snaps on the safety. How many rounds? Ahm, says the smart money, counting on your fingers. Let's see, you say aloud, the clip holds seven rounds plus one in the chamber if you're so inclined, so ahm, let's see, there should now be three in the clip and one round in the chamber. Sam abruptly ejects the clip downward into the upturned palm of his left hand and jacks the chambered round onto the picnic table, which circles like a dreidel and we watch it, fascinated, until it stops. Sam studies the clip. Three little cartridge cases are visible through the various inspection holes in the side of the clip. Four, Sam repeats as if to himself. Your hand descends into the heart of the trash and cans and bottles in the basket of the shopping cart. You sure you don't want the spare magazine? That's a three-hundred-dollar pistol, Sam says, as if suddenly lucid. What are you, you say, the shopping channel? Good price, Sam says as if to himself. Which was sixty dollars, you remind him. Where'd a schizophrenic shithead get a pistol such as this? Sam says, as if paranoid, as if to himself. The shopping channel? you suggest feebly. Oh, Sam says dully. You sure you don't want the spare, you say, having fished it up out of the trash. Sam shakes his head slowly. I haven't owned a gun since…Since…You don't own it yet, you state the obvious. Say, the smart money says, what's a progressive writer do all day? Same thing as a conservative one, Sam says, his tone duller than the finish on the monument commemorating your last war but one. Really? the smart money says, all day, stating the obvious? Or the impossible, Sam points out. Depends on your point of view. Say, Sam? you venture, about that sixty bucks…And put that thing away somewhere. Somebody might notice that you're sitting on municipal property in possession of a loaded firearm. I thought that was the idea, Sam observed dully. Sixty bucks sixty bucks sixty bucks, the smart money goaded. Riparian Sam placed the pistol in front of him on the picnic table. Stay over there where I can keep an eye on you. He reached into his rags in the vicinity of his breast and brought forth a handsome leather wallet, from which in due course emerged three crisp twenties. A good deal, he said, slipping the notes past one another again and again, to ensure there were but three of them. Here. And he hands them over. Oh, man, you say aloud, sixty less twenty percent is forty-eight dollars, divided by five is nine with three dollars left over. I'll bet Quincy down there to the *Uncertain Bollard* would be all too willing to build me a tenth martini for three dollars if I'd already scored the other nine from him. We got it made, we got it made, we got it made, another three days we got it made, another three days, way out into the future, as uncertainly goes, that we know more or less exactly what's going to happen, and therefore we know a great deal about what's not going to happen, although not everything that's not going to happen. I couldn't agree more, Riparian Sam said, calmly replacing the handsome billfold within the layers of his exoskeletal filth. Now, since I guess all I got to do is wait, I can say pretty much the same thing. You can say exactly the same thing, you say, assuming the draft-animal position at the handle of the shopping cart, exactly the same thing, I guarantee it. Yes, Sam says thoughtfully, as if to himself, as he fingers the expelled round into the clip. One can say with certainty what's probably going to happen, and what's probably not going to happen, but not with absolutely certainty, even if they both go the way you think they're going to go. Never, you agree. Not in a million years, Sam says. He fits the clip into the grip of the little automatic, whose barrel is shorter than its handle, chambers a round and sets the safety. Once its proximate chore is accomplished, Sam says as if to himself, this little pill will serve as the be-all and end-all of managed care. You push the cart a couple of feet, until now you are in the shade of the stunted Monterey pine, and between Sam and its trunk. Somebody has managed to not retrieve an empty beer can from the bed of weeds surrounding the tree's base. You do retrieve it. And you stomp it flat, as if thoughtfully, then place it atop the detritus in the basket of the shopping cart. You push the cart another foot. You stop and turn. Say Sam, you say, as if thoughtfully, where are you from, anyway? Sam, who has placed the pistol somewhere among the layers of his personal filth now gazes as if thoughtfully out over his watery domain. A moment passes. I can't remember, he finally answers truthfully. Just like where you're going, you tell him. And Riparian Sam is in all probably about to agree, though not really paying attention, when you drill him from behind. The shot snaps across the water, no louder than the crack of a bullwhip. Sam's head slumps forward quite gently, and you don't even have to help him, it eases down onto the inside of the elbow of his right arm like he's had two bottles of fortified wine on a warm day, like it's messed with his medication, which admixture is contraindicated anyway, it says so right on the five pages of instructions they hand out with it at the VA, and he looks just like he's slipped into a drowsy afternoon reverie. I don't know if your reputation is going to survive this, the smart money observes. But you're not having any of that. You bury the other .25 in the trash in the shopping basket and begin to wrangle the cart north along Terry A. Francois Boulevard. The rays of a late afternoon sun slant along the asphalt in front of you, left to right, west to east. A mile south, the shift whistle sounds at the Bethlehem shipyard.

NINE

SET ME UP, YOU SAY TO QUINCY, AS YOU EASE YOUR ADDLED integument onto the stool farthest from the front door of the Uncertain Bollard. Martini, high dry and Arctic, Quincy says, with a swipe of his rag over your little personal bartop hectare, and he spins a square of cocktail napkin in front of you. Boy oh boy oh boy, you say, aloud but more or less to yourself, sixty bucks. Less twenty percent that's forty-eight dollars and say, Quincy? Say, what? I been meaning to talk to you about that. About what? About how five goes into forty-eight nine times with three dollars left over? That it does, Quincy says, as he inverts a quart of *Andrei Rublev*, the well vodka, over his stainless steel cocktail shaker. So say I drink all nine of them here, you coyly advance while trying not to wheedle, you think you could throw me the tenth one for three? I've allowed for a twenty percent tip, you blandish. Quincy fakes the pour spout atop a quart of extra dry Vermouth toward the cap of the cocktail shaker, which he then immediately evacuates into the sink. Nine of what? he says, capping the shaker and giving it what for. Why, nine martinis, of course, you admonish him. The fuck I been drinking in here for twenty years? That's all very well and good, Quincy says, as he continues to give the shaker what for. But a martini in here is now six-fifty. How to convey the roar that rises through the column of my spine and bifurcates into both ears like a Blue Angel chandelle over the Alcatraz of my corpus callosum? Your over-reacting, suggests the smart money, though I, too, am shocked. A what in where is how much? you demand to know, like you're some kind of journalist, and Quincy, placing a frozen martini glass on the serviette in front you decants the shaker into it as he says, this puppy here, as of last week, is six-fifty. Is it any wonder that this society makes people crazy? you ask aloud, nay, shout. As Quincy visibly winces the smart money adds, is it any wonder that this society makes crazy people crazier? It's not society, Quincy says, as he defensively coaxes every last thickened drop into the surface tension that rises a full molecular layer above the actual rim of the martini glass, it's the economy. Fuck the economy, you calmly pronounce, drawing inner peace from the very sight of your first cocktail in three weeks, through the clear fluid of which filaments snake, like maleficent sea serpents guarding the two olives of doom. Give me a pencil, you meekly request in a shaken voice. Quincy complies, then goes about his business at the other end of the bar. Despite that he pours a generous drink, despite that he lets me drink in here in the first place, I'm cutting that bastard's tip back to gamma martinis plus point one five times gamma tips equals sixty bucks. Collect terms. Gamma bucks equals sixty bucks divided by one point one five equals $52.17. Six dollars and fifty cents divided into fifty-two dollars and seventeen cents is eight point one seven four. Round down to eight. The shaft. That's what it is. The economy is giving me the shaft. Not like the shaft you gave Riparian Sam, the smart money points out. I'm coming up one drink short on what I thought was a sure thing, you continue, ignoring all moral vectors, as usual, and secure in what is perhaps the least paranoid aspect of your self-awareness, which is the knowledge that the smart money only brings up moral vectors to tweak you. Quincy, you're shafting me, you say aloud. I don't make the rules around here, Quincy states the obvious. I'm just the morning man, six to two. No time for lunch? My customers eat my lunch for me. Don't change the subject. What do you want me to do, Quincy asks, showing just the least sign of impatience, make you pay up front? Now you're insulting me, you reply. Since when have I ever owed you a red cent for anything? I—you count the spondees on the bar with a forefinger—pay— my—bills. Cash and carry, Quincy notes mildly. That's right, you iambic fuck. Hey, Quincy says, laughing despite himself. No wonder I let you drink in here. It's a large wonder, in fact, observes the smart money. You stay out of this, you inadvertently respond aloud. Quincy looks around. You talking to me? He walks down the bar and shakes the remnants of the first cocktail into your glass, topping it off thereby, if perhaps with alcohol somewhat diluted with the water accrued from the melting ice. I am confronted with a dilemma, you declaim, and morose, I confront the morass. And your usual vista? Quincy asks, not unkindly. The underside of an overpass, you smile dreamily. Porous, gray, unyielding—although the odd heavy truck does make it tremble. That might certainly coax me from one alcoholic haze to the next, Quincy confirms, speaking personally. You nod distantly. The horrible present quakes with insubstantiality, the smart money whispers. The telephone rings behind the bar, next to the cash register. Quincy takes up the receiver, listens. Hiya babe, he says after a moment. Quincy lifts a foot and parks it along the edge of the sink under the bar, and toys with a stack of napkins there. No, no, he says, not busy. Your face burns. I enjoyed it, Quincy says. He catches the receiver between his shoulder and the side of his face. I don't want to know what your husband wants to know. You consider your cocktail. You breath in deeply, breath out slowly. And what, in the end, is solved? Nothing, says the smart money. If somebody had showed me a boat when I was ten, you theorize, my whole life may have been different. Different how, the smart money says, abruptly interrogatory, you mean you might have gone to sea with iron men in iron ships, with whom and therein to watch pornography, while intelligent machines did all the sailing? And all the loading and unloading? And all the hiring and firing? And all the evisceration of the union pension fund? The question seems relevant, you hedge. Inverting a highball glass, Quincy twists its mouth atop a stack of napkins, causing their edges to separate into a spiral. I haven't gotten enough of you, he says softly. That's too much information, you say to the smart money, not taking your eyes off your drink. Too much. You want to do something about it or not? Quincy asks the telephone. You touch the stem of the cocktail glass with the tips of the fingers of both hands, as if it were a delicate moment in time, as if you could handle a matter of delicacy in any way shape or form whatsoever. But seven drinks with the possibility of an eighth, you are brooding, as opposed to nine drinks with the possibility of a tenth, makes the difference between two to three days of satisfying oblivion at five to three drinks per day, and two to three days of a less than satisfying semi-oblivion at four to less than three drinks per day. A muddling stultification. Maybe you should repurpose your adulterous ways, Quincy is saying, and even the smart money is cringing inwardly. Except that inward is the one direction you don't want to go, that you really can't go. You lost that capacity a long time ago. Inward is dark, there really is not that much there, a few signposts, maybe, many of them splintered or even missing, just jagged stubs with bush clover and California poppies sprouting round them. And the lonely wind. This reminds you of the country. Forget the country, the smart money reminds you, you wouldn't last a day. Besides, most bars out in the county? They figure the martini for a fairy drink, you order one, they tell you so, and the next thing you know they're stomping you face down into a ditch out back. What a vision of America, you manage to croak. Finish that drink, the smart money advises, you'll feel better. You finish the drink. I no longer feel at home here, you say to nobody in particular. Customer, Quincy says off-handedly. he drops his foot from the edge of the bar sink to the floor. I gotta go. What? Sure. Another? he says, hanging up. You blink. It is written, the smart money says, and you repeat the remark, adding, all over my face. My opinion exactly, Quincy remarks, tossing the balance of the cocktail out of the shaker and into the sink. You hear about that couple, got themselves popped out at Land's End last week? A tremor ripples through your extra-pyramidals. I thought you had more self-control than that, the smart money remarks. Are the extra-pyramidals voluntary or not? you respond archly. Minding their own business, they were, Quincy says, as he drags the stainless beaker through the sinkful of ice. Surfer dude and his wife. Two kinds. You know, you say carefully, there was a couple of cops came to call under the bridge just this morning, wanting to know about that exact same case. Sounded like it, anyway. Oh yeah? Quincy says, evincing only mild interest, two cops came in here asking about whether I knew anything. Now your eyelids flutter. When? Yesterday. What, did those two people drink in here? The cops? The couple. Never heard of them, Quincy said, although, you know, if I still read a newspaper I mighta read about it. All you can do is grunt. Well, Quincy says, doing his thing with the vermouth, how many couples get popped for no reason out at Land's End? Ever think about that? Not many, you respond, especially with no reason. Come to think of it, Quincy says, adding a healthy dose of *Andrei Rublev* to the shaker, what

93

would be a good reason? Or any reason? I don't know, you shrug. They pissed somebody off? That's pretty pissed off, Quincy observes, capping the shaker. I had a friend once, he says. Went to high school with him. He shakes the shaker with vigor, another reason to drink in here, observes the smart money. Lot of these places, they got these husky kids working in there, they shake the shaker like they never jerked off in their life. He's out at Land's End with his kid one afternoon, just to look at the ocean. How old was the kid? I don't know, Quincy says thoughtfully. I was at the wedding, so he couldn't have been…He stops shaking the cocktail. In order to think, apparently. My friend was carrying him around, so maybe he wasn't walking yet. He resumes shaking. Came up from the beach and caught a guy breaking into his car. Guy turned around and shot him. Wow, you say, genuinely shocked. And the kid? Quincy pours. They found him sitting there between cars next to his father, unscathed. His father was dead. Jeeze, you say thoughtfully, that's superhero material. Huh? Quincy says, genuinely nonplussed. That kid could grow up to be, you know, a masked crimefighter. The martini topped off, Quincy screws the bottom half of the yet-to-be-emptied shaker into the ice-filled sink. Never thought of it that way, he says thoughtfully. It's more or less the initial plot device of *Batman*, the smart money tells you to tell him. The kid that grows up to be Batman witnesses the murder of his own father. Or both his parents, maybe. From then on, he's snakebit. So what's your excuse, Quincy asks, looking you in the eye. This guy knows too much, you council the smart money fearfully. He knows nothing, the smart money retorts with contempt. Good question, you say aloud, and I might ask you the same. I don't consider myself snakebit, Quincy says simply. And me? you ask. I was just kidding, Quincy lies easily. Just making conversation. Well, you repeat stubbornly, maybe those people at the beach pissed somebody off. Like you mean, maybe they interrupted a guy breaking into their car? Wouldn't that piss you off? Not enough to shoot somebody, Quincy replies. Oh, so you'd rather let him get the cops on you, send you to San Quentin? Folsom? Vacaville? Pelican Bay? Guy shoulda thought of that in the first place, Quincy states the obvious. Maybe he was desperate, you suggest. No shit, Quincy replies, desperate and stupid. Could be, you say thoughtfully. They ever catch the guy who killed your friend? Quincy shook his head. What about his kid? You mean, Quincy says, did the kid grow up to be Batman? You puff a little air through your lips, by way of expressing frustration. No, Quincy says. After the funeral, I lost track of him and the whole family. Later I heard his wife remarried and left town. So that kid had nobody to count on, you say, nobody. I guess so, says Quincy. Except his mama, maybe. What the fuck do you know, you say. Huh? Quincy says. Forget it, you say. Quincy studies you for a moment. After a longer moment he says thoughtfully, I guess you know from snakebit. Could be, you reply with mild acid. Could be. Well look who's here, a third voice says. Both you and Quincy turn and, Lo and behold, Quincy says, we were just talking about you. He turns to you. These the guys? These are the guys, you say cheerfully. They take adjacent stools at the far end of the bar, their backs to the door. And what was you saying, the younger of the two asks, about us. We were wondering if you were the same two cops who visited the two of us yesterday and the day before I guess it was, in the course of your investigation of that nice young couple who got popped out to the Land's End last week. How's your tinnitus? the older one abruptly asks you. Just a squallin' and a squealin', you manage to tell him. It sounds like somebody's tuning an AM radio way out in eastern Montana, where here's no stations. Jeeze, sympathizes the younger cop, who plainly doesn't believe you. It sounds like a kindergarten playground a half a block away, you persist, only it's not. It's in your head. See? the older one says to the younger one. You better start wearing those gun muffs. He turns back to the bar. Shamus, Jr., here, he takes target practice? He shakes his head. He won't wear the gun muffs. Thinks gun muffs are for pussies. That's okay, I assure him, because tinnitus is definitely not for pussies. That's true, Quincy says, I know a guy committed suicide behind his tinnitus. You gentlemen ready for a drink? Coffee, the older one says. Ginger ale, the younger one says. That's a lot of sugar, the older one tells him. Gun muffs, sugar, the younger one replies without humor, what are you, my mother? She told me to keep an eye on you, his partner replies easily. He straightens up and sits back from the bar as Quincy places a napkin in front of each of them. While we're on the subject, the older one says to nobody in particular, we think we may have found the guy's been going around town shooting people. Yeah? Quincy says, as he spritzes soda into a glass full of ice. I, who have ducked my chin low over the bar in order to suction the top layer of surface tension off the top of my martini with my lips, raise my eyebrows interrogatively. Which means they go front to back over the bar, parallel to its surface, instead of up and down, perpendicular to it. What's he got to say for himself? Quincy asks, as he stands the glass of ginger ale on the napkin in front of the younger cop. Not much, the older cop replies. How could he, Quincy says, retrieving a ceramic cup from the little dishwasher under the bar and placing it on the napkin in front of the older cop. There can't possibly be a rational explanation. Wait a minute. Did you say people? There's more than the two victims out at the beach? So it would seem, the older cop says. A corner of his upper lip lifts as he watches Quincy pour coffee. Even from the other end of the bar you can smell that the coffee has been sitting on the burner since six-thirty this morning, but, Yeah, you get your oar in, you were only talking about some couple out to the beach when you talked to me. The younger cop is watching you wordlessly, and he doesn't touch his ginger ale. That's true, the older cop says. Ballistics makes out we're up to four, maybe five gunshot victims. He waits patiently as Quincy sets a little stainless pitcher of cream, a spoon, and a chrome-topped glass dispenser full of white sugar on the bar in front of him. We got the gun for sure, we got a suspect, maybe. That's a relief, you row your oar. Guys going around the city popping people off, it makes everybody nervous. Like the Zebra killers. Remember them? The cop takes up the spoon, starts stirring, and upends the sugar dispenser over the vortex. Sugar cascades into his coffee, he's stirring and watching, everybody's watching it. Damn, honey, he says to the coffee, you're older than I thought. Hell, Quincy says, as if mesmerized by the cascade of white sugar, I remember the Zebra case. Black guys, you say, as if startled, going around town shooting white people at bus stops. Completely at random. Killed five or six people. They killed sixteen people, the older cop says to his coffee. What? you say, aghast. At a minimum, he adds, setting the sugar dispenser back on the bar at last. I never heard that, Quincy says. Not many people heard that, the older cop says. But some authorities think it could have been as many as seventy. They killed a lot of homeless, hitchhikers, people with no antecedents, as we say down at the Department of Unexplained Deaths. Is that your department? Quincy asks. No, the older cop says, pausing over the rim of his coffee cup. We work out of the Department of Explained Deaths. Exclusively. He sips once, twice, a third time. Damn, he says, setting the cup down. You may be old, but this coffee's older. I made it fresh this morning, Quincy protests. The younger cop glances at his watch. Still, he does not speak. An interesting aspect of the Zebra murders? The older cop dabs a corner of his napkin at the corner of his mouth and looks at it. What broke that case was a snitch, he says. What broke the snitch was a tip that came from the old 500 Club at the corner of Haight and Fillmore. Quincy frowns, trying to remember something. The young cop assumes a respectful attitude, as toward a body of knowledge to which he has no direct access. Last time I saw that place open, I say, it was surrounded by cop cars. An array of them fanned through the intersection, the hood of each one pointed at the front door of the bar, which held down the northeastern corner. Every door on every vehicle stood open and behind each door crouched a cop with a drawn weapon. Shotgun, pistol, whatever, that weapon was pointed at the front door of the 500 Club. That's the place, the older cop said. You're older than I thought. They say everybody who drank at that bar got handed a foot of duct tape as they came in the door, so they could tape their piece up under the bar. That way, when the cops came in and frisked everybody, a regular occurrence, everybody was clean. See? I smiled. Yeah, the older cop said. It was a rough neighborhood, back in the day, Quincy concluded. What were you doing there? Drinking, I shrugged. I mighta known, Quincy said. Without a doubt, the older cop said. What do we owe you? Quincy waved a hand. The two cops stood off their respective barstools. A cop went undercover, I said to the bar. He drank in the 500 Club every night, and eventually he got the tip that broke the case. That's the way I heard it, anyway. That's nothing to do with the case at hand, the older cop said. He ducked his head. But—you know?—there is an odd coincidence. What's that? Well, like the case at hand, and with the exception of that nasty incident with the machete, all of the Zebra murders were committed with a thirty-two. For no good reason, and lots of bad ones, I found this morsel disconcerting. Really? I managed lamely, I had no idea. Look it up on Wikipedia, came the suggestion. I...don't have a computer, came the response. After a short pause, the younger cop laughed. Quincy joined in. Finally, even the older cop, after a look around, gave me a shrug, a smile, and then a laugh. Then the laughter died out. Another pause. A lotta loose ends to that case, the older cop finally said, and he said it to me. Some cases are like that. He laid a five on the bar. No charge, Quincy said quickly. The older cop waved this off. Thanks, he said to Quincy. See you around, he said to me. Then they left.

TEN

THE FLAG HAS BEEN THERE FOR SIX DAYS. ONE DAY TO GO. YOU shouldn't go to work, the smart money said, not for a while, let alone tomorrow or next week. Maybe not even this year. I gotta have a drink, you say, looking at the flag. It's not a flag, actually, just a bit of rag threaded through a corner at the far end of the chain link fence, right next to the sign that says No Bicycles, No Pedestrians, No Hitchhiking. It almost looks as if the wind could have deposited it there, just like the rest of the trash all around it; but in fact it's threaded through and around the corner in such a way as to leave human intervention unquestionable. At least take a month off, maybe even a year off. Let's ride the rails down to Santa Barbara, check out some sun for a change. This perpetual winter they got around here is getting me down. After forty years? Don't you think it's about time? You talk like you weren't around for that dream last night. I was there. But hey, it's only since we found that refrigerator carton that you've been able to dream at all. Snug as a louse in year-old long johns. Who wouldn't dream? Why is it always 'we' when it comes to finding refrigerator cartons, and 'you' when it comes to dreaming? The super-ego doesn't allow dreaming. Dreaming is counterproductive to the inter-ests of the Combine. Dreaming is left up to the id. The super-ego is in charge of refrigerator cartons. Thanks for the softball question. What's with the moving legs? We're going to lose this carton. It could be pouring rain and we'd be snug for a month. Best cardboard in the lower forty-eight. Only those boxes the fishermen use for ice in Alaska are superior. Hey. Speaking of Alaska—. We'll find another. The Combine breeds refrigerator cartons like year-old long johns breed lice. Like ids breed superegos. Like ids breed psychotics, you mean. Can a person simultaneously contribute to the efficiency of the Combine and not be psychotic? Are you kidding? They have their own newsletter. Chat room. Forum. Chatter forum. Must be loud in there. Mostly it's about blocking weirdos. Here's Market Street already. Take Cyril Magnin to O'Farrell and transect the Tenderloin. To see how the other half resuscitates. You got to bear down, pal. Are you sure about this? One's thirst informs one's destiny. Walking is good exercise, and exercise is good for thinning the lipids. What did they tell you at the VA? Start thinning your lipids or we'll take off that leg and use it for an ashtray—which reminds me: no smoking. Straight-up medical advice, maggots to clean the wound, and spagum moss to stanch the bleeding. All the world is uppercase G God's own dispensary. You got off the troop ship and walked Market to O'Farrell with your seabag on your shoulder and just about here is where your Zippo lighter fell out of the bag's mouth and she picked it up and returned it to you. That's how you met. Is it true love, after a tour of duty? Back when you used to kill people for free? No, no. All in the line of duty. You killed one for free just the other day. No, no. In the line of duty. You don't even remember her name, do you. I never knew her name. No, no. The one who picked up the lighter. I never used to smoke, either. Listen. You can lie to the VA doctor about smoking, but you can't lie to me. Don't change the subject: what was her name? If you were in front of my eyes instead of behind them, I'd shift them away from you. Evasive, like. You know I don't like that

word, evasive. Yes, yes, the smart money said tiredly, you like
to confront the world head-on. When you look up that term in
the dictionary, the smart money pointed out, the usage example is a remark by one Henry A. Kissinger. "I have wondered
since whether it would have been wiser to meet the issue
head-on." My uppercase G God, you say, now he wonders
about it. Which culture was it, you might explain to me, that
Mr. Kissinger failed to smash head hyphen on? He was probably referring to his limited freedom in traveling abroad due
to various international arrest warrants issued by various legal
entities throughout the developed world. A little fucking late
for certain blighted canopies, you adduce bitterly. You still
haven't told me her name, the smart money observes tartly.
Okay, okay...I can't remember it. Surely it's somewhere, in
your slough, and fecund, in the muck. Lingering like a doubt.
You're convinced this is a matter of destiny. Is that not upper-
case D? Only if you over-rate it. Quod the author of *The
Anatomy of Melancholy*, "Marriage and hanging go by destiny." Melancholy indeed. Well, the latter seems to be locked,
in a matter of speaking. There's the Mitchell Brothers
Theater, likely the most famous and long-lived palace of porn
in the lower forty-eight. Ah, Artie and Jim. Good Irish lads,
the one killed the other, I've forgotten which. Slain and Able,
as the great S. Clay Wilson used fondly and often to refer to
them, the one dead, the other free to porn again. A veritable
porn again Christian. Aren't we the lively guest among the
arts-as-practiced-by-entrepreneurs today. If you had a back
I'd slap it. So many puns, so much money. Think of it. And
there's the old Ye Rose and Thistle. Another pornographic
venue. The first Sam Shepard play I ever saw was upstairs
over that bar. They had a little set of bleachers on casters, so
they could move the audience around, if the dramaturge were

so inclined. Like the bleachers. So inclined? So many puns, so much money. What a gig. Think of it. They sat maybe forty people, maybe four rows high, ten people wide. Could it have been five rows high, eight people wide? Thirty-eight plus two handicap, I believe is the fire code. Any more seats than that, your talking smoke detectors, clearly marked fire exits, panic hardware on the doors, independently circuited emergency lighting....When the show started, the dramaturge had to scamper downstairs and beg the bartender to turn off the jukebox for the duration. Every once in a while there'd be a fight about that, and the audience would have to rush downstairs to restore order. The ones eager to fight for art, that is. Not too many of those. Bit of an intellectual crowd. Pussies, you mean. You ordered a double Jameson rocks and nursed it, waiting at the bar for the rope over the narrow stair to be dropped so the audience could file up and take its seat, if there were just the one person. You still had the Zippo, mainly because of the habit you'd developed right away in the service, to while away the ninety percent of the time you spent waiting there, too, of snapping the lighter just so between the thumb and first two fingers of your left hand, which flipped open the lighter, and snapping the middle finger of your left hand over your thumb and against the serrated wheel, which scratched the flint, whose sparks lit the wick. With a flick of your wrist, the lighter closed and extinguished itself. Over and over again, you'd do this. One night, the bartender came over and offered to buy the drink if you'd stop fucking with your cigarette lighter. Music to my ears, you told him. There was always somebody around this habit would annoy, but usually they would offer to fight instead of bribe you. Do you remember the name of the show? Sure. *Killer Head*. And you said it wasn't pornographic? No, I didn't, but I will now. So many puns, so much—. It was a ten-minute monologue. Lights come up on a cowboy-looking guy strapped into a chair. Can't remember whether it had casters on it. Can't remember whether he was blindfolded, or hooded, but he might have been. I think he was. The setup reminded me of Beckett's *Endgame*, that's for sure. Clove, you know, in his black shades on a throne with casters. Anyway, the throne in *Killer Head* is an electric chair, the guy in the chair, who has no name, is waiting to be electrocuted, he's all alone in the show, as in death, and he delivers himself of a ten minute monologue, all to do with breaking a horse using a martingale. Which is—? Doesn't make any difference. Sure, but—which is…? It's an adjustable strap that connects a horse's chin to the girth strap, in order to inhibit its tossing its head or, presumably, its rider. The cowboy delivers himself of this recondite squib about martingales, then—zap, he's electrocuted, and blackout. That's it? Show's over. Huh. Where was this again? Right over there. Now a porn venue. Neighborhood's full of them. Not a bad bar. Theater was upstairs. When? You have to think about this. I still had the lighter. From the service. So you still smoked. I never smoked. Look, you can lie to the doctor at the VA about your smoking, but I'm your superego, for chrissakes. Some of you is. What's that? Some of you is my superego. And the rest of me? Pure asshole. That's what it takes, to ride herd on the id. Gee, haw, cut up Polk. Van Ness is unneccesarily thrashy. Eight lanes in two directions, buses…But, say, regardless of when you saw it, could you not regard the fact that you saw it at all as portentous? Of what? Of your destiny? Ah! You lick the envelope! In retrospect, you mean? Why, in prospect, even. In the moment, you mean? In that, as well as this. It's like—it's like you go to the phone to call someone, pick it up, and as you're touching the tones a voice on the line asks what's going on and, and—it's the very person you were trying to contact! What is? Oh beloved, you say, serendipitous kismet! My lower-case g god, control yourself. You're getting carried away. But—is it not spring? You look around, paranoid. I always become ill, you say with suspicion, at the change of season. What you perceive as illness, the smart money points out, others perceive as an elevation of the spirit. Lower-case s? you ask. The smart money has to think about this. Possibly, he finally allows. So what do they know, therefore, you are able to conclude. Ah, the Hemlock Bar. *Conium & Cicuta*, take your choice, my dear Sophocles, they will both short your circuit. No, that would be Socrates, I believe, who was condemned for corrupting the minds of Athenian youth. A worthy end, if you're asking me, no matter the nationality, but I stand corrected. After all, one has read the *Crito*. Not a bad name for a law firm. So many declamations, so much money. Would that it were so. Everybody would be rich. Wherein the aforementioned and foredoomed Socrates lamely attempts to enforce the edict of reason over the hogwash of cultural values. That will be the day. A symptom of decadence, would not you think? What, reason? No, no, rather, the predominance of so-called cultural so-called values over so-called reason. You mean like, upper-case D Democracy? Precisely. The opinion of the many, versus the actual truth of the matter—triumphalism, in a word. The more I talk to you, the more I need a drink. Of hemlock? No! Of martini. If you had the choice, between the electric chair and hemlock, which would you chose? I would chose the middle way, the just path, the channel between the Scylla of hemlock and the Charybdis of electrocution—behold the martini. Which costs, now, six-fifty. Plus tip, et voilà hi ho, it's off to work we go. Which brings us, by way of the far end of Polk Street, a veritable memory lane best left for another time as the mind is cleared for duty, and finally, west on Sacramento Street to the southeastern corner of Lafayette Park. Finally. That'll be the day. The westerly is up, ruffling the neglected grass at the eastern end of the dog run. Nasturtiums quiver along the chainlink fence at the corner of the lower tennis court, and there's a dirt path there, somewhat muddy always, despite the dry climate, which heads north along both tennis courts. Today there's a teacher with a machine that launches green balls over the net in the direction of a young student, who willy-nilly bats them everywhere. A number of balls are to be seen in the long grass that falls abruptly from the path to the backs of various apartment buildings, which block any view of Gough Street but screen the park's habitués from the noise of its incessant traffic. As you walk along the fence you stoop and toss balls over the top of it, exercise is good for your lipids. The tennis teacher, who is a young man and fit, bored but cheerful with his lot or vice versa, which in either case does not bear much scrutiny as work, though for it he is remunerated nonetheless, thanks you for the first one, dribbles with his racquet into submission such balls as come his way, there's no rush, the others resume their willy-nillyness, and the court is littered with them. The machine has ceased to cough and now he hits a ball over the net to the little girl, a lob, you think they call it, and, watching this feckless performance, it's hard to believe that organized sports pave the road to fascism, because, for one thing, this sport they're disporting is barely organized. Maybe they agreed on a time, but that's about it. And a price, and now we're beginning to get organized. So maybe that's it. That's the crack in the door. But these thoughts, too, pass. There's a little knoll to climb and now you're in a clearing. There's a woman with each elbow clasped in the hand of the opposite

arm, and from one of the hands dangles the loop of a leash.
She's watching a dog as it sniffs its way among the various coy-
ote and monkey flower bushes lining the perimeter of the
clearing. A bluff overlooks the west side of this clearing, tall
eucalyptuses tower above everything and their leaves clatter
in the westerly like the syllables in *clafouti*. She allows herself
a grimace in greeting, then returns her attention to her dog,
not entirely, however, taking her eye off you. Hey, you want to
say, I'm the guy who was lobbing tennis balls over the fence
back there just now, to save that guy with the cabled sweater
draped over his shoulders the trouble of having to exit the
gate on the opposite side of the tennis court to trudge all the
way around to the side of the hill and round up thirty or forty
stray balls cause there's no way that petulant child he's being
paid to keep out of her parent's apartment for two hours
would do it for him or even help him do it, so don't be looking down your nose at me like I'm a formidably intimidating
street person with no credentials, wherewithal or resources
other than his feet and an innate ability to supplicate.
Resculpt your demeanor, the smart money says, its a normal
reaction to the likes of you. You're right, I forget to recollect
myself, you'd think I'd be used to it by now. Cringe onward.
At the far end of the clearing there's a path that rises through
the hectoring eucalyptuses, into whispering tall pines, through
which there comes into view a magnificent northerly vista of
the San Francisco Bay, Alcatraz dead center, little ferryboats
pursing their festive rhumb lines, framed by the proscinium of
a pair of the most magnificent apartment buildings in San
Francisco, along the north side of Washington Street, the tops
of which feature stunning penthouses, no doubt, I've always
been curious to visit them, and in fact waited in a car in the
circular drive of one of them while a companion scored for

heroin in one of them, in one or another of the epochs of the Quaternary Period, I think it was, more nostalgia, it must be true that the older one becomes the more the mind fills with the unnecessary detritus to be found uniquely on either side of the wake of time as experienced by the human mind, although one does wonder what any dog finds so interesting on either side of a given path, but stay on task, today is the day you contribute to the efficiency of the Combine if you but stay on task, and thus enable to yawn the Martini Gate to the Ancient City of Oblivia. There's a bench from which to contemplate all these marvels, Alcatraz, the bay, the ferry boats, Marin County and the villas of Belvedere beyond the white caps tossed up by an ebb falling under the westerly. The bench is halfway along the path, as it meanders the shoulder of the park above Washington Street. And next to this bench is a trash can, incongruously, perhaps, because it usually smells of rotting sandwiches and bagged dog feces, but there it sits. And on the end of the bench closer to the garbage can, you take a seat. Its odor is nothing to you, who reek more forcefully than any but the rankest poubelle, and in fact in this circumstances acts as camouflage. You have the flag with you, unthreaded from the chainlink fence perhaps two hours ago, and now you attach the flag to the handle on the garbage can with a simple overhand knot, as if idly, as if someone had lost it and you'd found it and you're leaving it conspicuously behind, in case its owner should think to look for it here. After contemplating the view for a while, you raise the lid on the can and have a look. The envelope is there, somewhat crumpled, and beneath two or three layers of bagged dog feces, the remains of bagged lunches—never any bottles or cans, which are retrieved by scavengers within an hour of their deposit. The envelope is addressed to somebody, somewhere. This address is meaningless. The envelope also has a return address, however, and it's the address of the person whose photograph is to be found inside the envelope. That's all. The five thousand dollars will be waiting in Union Square, folded into a newspaper, later, after one more step.

ELEVEN

THERE'S A HAWAIIAN BAR WAY OUT GEARY BOULEVARD WHERE oncologists go to relax. I'm not kidding. There's a roof made out of pseudo-fronds over the bar, tiki chain-saw sculptures, leis draped over the light fixtures, and all the slack key guitar a customer can stomach while downing some rum concoction and eavesdropping arcane persiflage concerning angiogenesis inhibitors etc. In fact it's a lot like sitting in a cafe surrounded by people speaking a language you don't speak. The effect is to permit the mind a great deal of space—in a word, the effect is desirable. It's a long walk from Lafayette Park, nearly four miles. The way to enjoy it is to walk straight out Sacramento to Arguello, jog left to Clement, then way all the way out Clement until you cross 38th Avenue, at which point you duck one block over to Geary and you're there. Sacramento is boring, but there's not much traffic. Clement, on the other hand, teems with synecdoches of every country in Asia. China and Japan are represented, of course. But also Burma, Vietnam, Laos, Russia, Korea, Thailand. There's a bar with belly dancing and seventeen different kinds of raki from Israel, Turkey, Iraq—every country around the Mediterranean that brews booze....The savor is of unknown spices tinged with the reek of booze, of the backwash from yesterday's eel tanks, of coffees and teas, of newsprint and fried electronics, of unknown vegetables on display in balsa crates or rotting in the gutter, of stores selling live koi and extended clown triggerfish and monkey-face eels. There's even an excellent used bookstore, the largest in the city. Dim sum, catfish wraps, jicama and papaya salad, duck every which way including loose, Irish beer, Indian beer, Thai beer, Chinese beer, black Japanese beer on draft....That last five thousand dollars had you shitting blood before it was over with, the smart money reminds you as you're crossing Sixth Avenue. Indeed, you reply, that was fresh. You stop to have a look at the bargain bins on the sidewalk in front of Green Apple Books. It was also three months ago. Cleared up right away. That's not the way I remember it. If you can remember anything at all, it's not gone forever. Hey, here's everything Michael Connelly ever wrote. And Molière. Has it really been three months? No wonder I'm thirsty. When's the last time you read a book. I've been reading ever since my computer died. You never had a computer. That's right. How was it, exactly, that this binge mentality came about? If it hasn't to do with erratic funding, I'm sure I don't know. That fish tank store used to be an open-air newsstand. Had every periodical published in English, I think. Those were the days. How much money did you ever spend in there? I bought *Time* magazine there, once, just to read for myself the article about how taking LSD made people stare at the sun until they went blind. Oho, that was a good one. Makes the internet look like the Nether Pole of Probity. And you haven't had a good laugh since. Three months circling the Cul-de-sac of Thirst would make Santa Claus humorless. Such a distant memory hardly qualifies as a binge, does it. Not if you can't remember it. Three months! It's not simple deprivation, it's strict parole. It's the difference between mere inconvenience and total derailment. And yet, with the latter you do flirt. And just exactly how far do you ever get, flirting? We've gotten as far as this Levantine grocery, here, which reeks of olives and fennel. It never ceases to amaze us that we can smell anything at all. One thing about the people on the sidewalk in this neighborhood, they don't bat an eye at the odd blunderbuss of aroma. They probably think I'm comestible, in one way or another. Momentarily, at least. Long enough for you to slip past forever. Olfactory cloaking device. To wash or not to wash—that is to say, to put the olfactory cloaking device at risk—isn't even a question. But to drink...That's not a question either. Lookit that row of ducks. How do they get them to look like that? How do they get people to buy them when they look like that? You are not, I believe, the target audience. This entire street, as a matter fact, will continue merrily into the future without the like of you. Or even the dislike of you. You are invisible to them, a non-entity, precisely the definition of cipher. A zero. Zeroness. Zeroicity. All the easier to get by with. Not so much as a personal photograph on the internet. Almost impossible to affect. We could jog over to the park. I'm not jogging anywhere. Thinning your lipids today, that's for sure. Look at the nice big picture window on the front of that supermarket across the street. Looks like they clean it every day. Indeed it does. So: are we being followed, or not? If we are, they're more insipid than we. Probably wore their asses out with this four-mile route. We're only three miles into it, the pussies. Unless... Unless what? Unless they already know where we're going? What, so they can just wait for us there? Look, look, look, insists the smart money. I'm looking. How many people in this town do you think have heard about this Hawaiian bar where oncologists go to unwind? You have to shake your head. Damn few, if it's an inside thing. But, you say, that's precisely the kind of obscure detail a cop would pride himself on knowing. Just like you do, supposed the smart money. You have to nod your head.

Damn, says the smart money. What? you say. You look and act just like you're on the phone. Well I'm not on the phone, you say, as the blood rushes to your face, I'm just trying to be a perfectly normal paranoid schizophrenic whose mesolimbic flow of dopamine presents him with no prospect more diminutive than the odd if resplendent alcoholic stupor. Alcoholic stupor is not a co-morbid condition, the smart money observes calmly, like depression or anxiety or paranoia. No, you say, quite aloud, it's a palliative! A perfectly normal-looking woman abruptly pulls a U-turn right in front of you, and power walks in the opposite direction. Seeing that the light is red at the intersection of 8th, she takes an unhesitant hard left and crosses Clement. The other two or three hundred people within earshot merely glower. Now look what you've done, the smart money says. The lifetime occurrence of substance abuse among your sort of fuckup is about forty percent. You have a better chance of committing suicide than the average cellist, who censuses the highest suicide risk of any desk in the string section, which in turn censuses the highest of any section in the orchestra, and your nervous system should have collapsed completely some ten or twelve years ago. You're afraid of people, the open-air markets, any medicine you haven't prescribed yourself, women, girls, boys, dogs, yogurt and steam-powered automobiles. There is a reflection in that window who seems inordinately interested in you, you say. Where? The smart money is immediately alert. It's a Chinese-looking guy. He's looking out the door of that medicine shop. So he is. But, all in all, everybody on the street has become aware of you, now that you're shouting questions and answers at yourself. I want a drink. Did we drink that whole fifty bucks, the other…Was that yesterday? It was this morning. No, it was two weeks ago. But your theoretical Social Security check arrived just after, and you have not managed to drink it all up. So much for a fixed address. A little soup might do you a world of —. Potato chips at the bar will be sufficient, thank you. Hawaiian potato chips? Maybe two bags. Don't you worry about how they increase your heart rate? I worry about how everything else doesn't increase my heart rate. Life stimulates only the amygdallae. That guy's Chinese, he probably runs that medicinal herb place, he might even be the doctor himself. He might have something that will help you. And before you know it, you are seated before a counter heaped with prepackaged herbal sachets, a pan scale, a cash register of course. The lower part of the counter is glass, and within it are all manner of medicaments satisfying to contemplate, chief among them a big flask of snake wine sealed with wax. The guy behind the counter asks you a number of questions designed to make you comfortable, designed to make you think this guy is really interested in your condition, concerned about you as an individual, and your *chi* energy. As he's questioning you he's got your left wrist in his right hand and three fingers of his left hand on the inside of your wrist, one on each pulse, two of which are unknown to Western medicine. There's a very young girl on a stool behind the counter next to the guy, and she's writing Chinese characters down one side of a page and back up the other side in a huge ledger of the sort you'd normally associate with double-entry bookkeeping, and she's writing as fast as the questions come and your answers go. Age? Sixty-something. Smoke? Never got the habit. Must you continue to lie about that? the smart money says, just as the Chinese guy says, I think not. He says it in Chinese, however, and the girl writes it down. They think you're not grokking the gist of these characters which, upside down, look like road-kill scorpions. But you're so paranoid you're speaking perfect Chinese. So the guy behind the counter, you realize, can tell that you used to smoke by the metabolic telegraphy available to his expertise via his fingertips. His fingertips gently knead the inside of your wrist until he periodically readjusts the relation of the three fingers to your three pulses, it's like there are not a few figurative patterns he must assess. He adjusts them again, closes his eyes, and waits. The girl lifts her pen from the ledger. There comes a whine from your jejunum. Liver? he asks. No problem. I think otherwise, he replies, and she quickly writes it down. Blood in the urine? Only after a beating. How about in your stool? Did I ever piss blood in my stool? He does not dignify this with a response. Instead he waits. The pen hovers above the page. How did you know about the blood in the stool, you finally ask. He says something and the girl writes it down. Sleep? Not much. Through the glass on the countertop you can see the eyes of a snake, coiled amongst a number of his pickled ilk in the jar of liquor. While his brethren attend to other things, this one snake is watching you. What proof is that stuff? you ask aloud. The guy behind the counter ignores this. Gallstones, no, bladder infection, no, painful urination, no, shortness of breath, yes, a little. Medications? None. Unless you count alcohol. He nods. He counts alcohol, the smart money concludes. So do I, you say aloud. He releases your wrist and makes a little speech to the girl, who writes it all down. Strange they didn't ask me my name, you realize, watching the figures reel down and up the page. It's a very fat book and she's more or less in the middle of it. A large rubber band corrals the previously filled pages. The girl looks up and says Three dollars. You're startled. You blink. I beg her pardon, you say to nobody in particular. Three dollars, she repeats, closing the book. The Chinese guy leans down under the counter and produces a package covered in calligraphy, with a picture of Kuan Yin, maybe, and some gilded filigrees that look like brush-stroke bamboo leaves. He waits. The girl waits. Three dollars, they want, the smart money says, for whatever it is in that package. If it fixes the least little thing that is wrong with you, the smart money points out, that's pretty cheap. If it even makes a dent, you agree, and you fork over three of the five singles in your singles stash, to be discovered when the coroner goes through your clothes. She takes the money and gives it to the guy and the guy hands her the package. She wraps the package up in two pages of a Chinese language newspaper, using a clever and very quick manipulation of folds to seal the package without tape or string, and hands it to you. Once a day, she says in English, same time every day. You take the package and stand up from the wooden stool and it's only then that you notice that two women and an ancient old man have been patiently waiting while seated on a row of chairs immediately, claustrophobically against the wall behind you. You're hardly past the first one when she takes her place on the stool, rolls up her sleeve, and places her wrist on the mousepad atop the countertop. The young girl turns a page in the big book and resumes her seat. A fourth person, an old man, turns sideways as he enters the narrow shop, so as to slip past you as you're blocking the door. No visible reaction to your reek clouds his features. He puts each hand in its opposite sleeve and bows to the room in general before taking a seat. The round of perfunctory questions and murmured answers begins. You're on the sidewalk. The sun is out and it's uncustomarily warm for the Lake District. You're in a daze, you realize, but it's nothing to do with the weather. That guy, the smart money knows, that guy back there? That's the first time you've been touched by another human being in…Maybe a year? you respond absently. I'll bet it's more like five, the smart money says. I can't remember. It could be ten for all I know, you say. Or care. Oh? Then why do you feel so strange? the smart money says. Because it's the first time anybody's touched me in howsoever long, you're the one who brought it up, you say, and it's that simple. Did you see that snake? I saw snakes, plural. He flicked his tongue. Listen, the smart money suddenly shouts, *don't invent problems.* Okay? You hold up the package. What are we supposed to do with this? Once a day, she said, whatever it is. What if I have to cook it, you say, what then? Guess you wasted three bucks, the smart money supposes. Maybe it's something you're just supposed to eat. You find yourself at Clement and 17th. There's a municipal trash can on the corner, of the type that has a top and a door, so only the city can access the trash within. That's the theory, anyway, and it's a flawed theory. You put the package on the top of the trash can. You unwrap the outer layer. It smells sweet. Cloyingly sweet. You unwrap the inner layer. It's a bar of soap, the smart money realizes. So it is, you say, not touching it. Rose-scented soap, the smart money guesses. I'll be a son of a bitch, you say. You look back down Clement Street. The commercial strip has faded, it's mostly residential now, with the odd grocery, yoga studio, and dry cleaner. The apothecary is ten or twelve blocks east. It isn't worth it, that walk, just to get our money back. It's ten blocks back, maybe twelve, a big fight maybe, maybe not, and then ten or twelve blocks back to where we started from. A total of twenty to twenty-two blocks of walking, plus the fight. A deal of energy. You touch your breast, where the envelope is stashed on top of the breast of your long johns and underneath both of your shirts, as well as the overcoat. There's five grand, the smart money says, just waiting to be earned. A bar of soap, you say. Somebody, at long last, said what had to be said. I guess, the smart money sighs, that's one way of looking at it. You'd have thought, you say, that at least he'd have prescribed some nettle tea. To cleanse the liver. Isn't that what they're supposed to give you, to cleanse the liver? Maybe he

thinks your liver is hopeless, the smart money suggests, like you
do. You consider this. He could tell I used to smoke, you
remember. Not even the VA has figured that out, the smart
money points out—although they're waiting, I suspect, for
some mutant cells to betray your mendacity. The VA has all the
time in the world, you agree. They got a cancer for mighty nigh
everything, the smart money says, but sixty percent of all cancer is directly attributable to smoking. Doesn't that mean, you
ask shrewdly, I still got a forty per cent chance of fooling them?
I guess so, allows the smart money. You still got the cancer,
though, I remind us. *You* still got the cancer, the smart money
says. Not me. You. If any doubt lingers as to whether or not I'm
a figment of your imagination, or even of your brain chemistry,
the smart money reminds me, wait till you get the cancer. A
bank of fog has risen high over the Richmond, maybe a quarter
of a mile to the west. It represents an absence of sunlight and a
ten or even a fifteen degree drop in temperature. The tea-rose
colored bar of scented soap is able to hold down the printed tis-
sue and the two pages of Chinese-language newspaper that it
came wrapped in, for the moment; but the loose edges have
begun to waver in the chill moving inland in advance of the fog.
Soon the sheets of paper will turn into sails. They will take
flight, and the bar of soap will tumble to the sidewalk. To be
overcome by filth. You get the cancer, the smart money assures
you, you're going to be all by yourself. All alone. I can't wait to
savor the difference, you say aloud.

TWELVE

THE HAWAIIAN BAR, WHERE DISPORT ONCOLOGISTS AND THEIR groupies, is under new management, and the new management ask you to leave on account of the stink. No hygiene, no service. So you drag your bones on down Geary until it turns to Point Lobos Avenue, whence you turn south into Sutro Heights Park. There, on a cliff-top bench looking southwest over The Great Highway and the Esplanade, you withdraw the photograph from the now sweat-stained envelope. It's a woman. If you don't count the incident of a few months ago, wherein a woman got in between you and your job, and you don't, this is a first. Of course, you imagine, a woman can get into a bad way with the wrong people just as easily as a man can, but, still, this is a first. Ask me if I care, you say to the photograph. I'd like to remind you, the smart money reminds you, that the verb imagine and all its declensions, in particular the nominative forms, as well as any noun forms and any derivatives thereof, such as, in your dreams, or, I imagine it to be so, or even one imagines it to be so, are, will be, and have been, for a very long time, the sole discretion of the smart money, hereinafter known as The Proprietor. Your extrapyramidals contort until your face is a parody of itself. You thought we already had this discussion. Think of the smart money as a Kantian object, the smart money maintains, a soulless monad whose existence is intuited only by

the intellect and not perceived by the senses. Your extrapyramidals are not released. Especially other people's senses, you
manage, spittle flying. Also called Thing-In-Itself, not precisely
the soul, that cannot be known through perception, although its
existence can be demonstrated. No? A last twist of all the neu-
ral pathways throughout the musculature between the bones of
the face and their fleshy excrescences. Why didn't I think of
that! Come to think of it, why didn't I remember it? I've known
it all along! But yes! you exclaim. Of course! The pathways are
released. The smart money formally apologizes. Sorry, it says, as
if merely smoothing the front of its shirt, the pleats of which are
actually the runnelettes of your brain, I just had to walk that
dog on the cortical asphalt of your brain. Where else would you
walk it? you ask sensibly. You have a point, the smart money
somewhat begrudgingly admits. Perhaps three hundred feet
below the lip of the cliff, which is just ten yards from the bench,
a motorcycle accelerates down the grade from the Cliff House
and onto the flat expanse of the Great Highway. A seagull is lifted up the face of the cliff by a thermocline until it is at eye level
with you. A swift, comprehensive glance determines that you
are not yet food, despite smelling like it, and the bird, too, glides
south. Oh destiny, you recognize, why do you wait to claim me?
Yes, the smart money unexpectedly agrees, and there's nothing
for it. You consider the photograph. She's perhaps thirty?
Perhaps. An intelligent look about her. Yes. Not all that comfortable with being photographed. Apparently. Yet, accepting it.
You think she knew she was being photographed? That's an
interesting distinction. I couldn't say. You? I think not. If one
thought so, then she perhaps knows the person who knows you.
Nobody knows me. Stick to the point. That would complicate
things. I think so. May I ask what has spurred this intemperate
spate of introspection? Um, The Great Martini Famine? Quite

possibly. Nevertheless, in retrieving the envelope you've accepted the job, you've got a week to perform, within three days you get paid, and that's the beginning and the end of it. You don't give a damn who this person is, or why he/she/it has come to this particular crossroad. The envelope itself is addressed to the attention of Mr. Mifune Sibaabwe, Chamber of Commerce, 14, Al-Fayyum St., Abuja, Nigeria. There's a cover letter. They're always the same. Dear Mr. Sibaabwe. This is to be thanking you very much for your contribution. As you can see by the accompanying photo, the plastic surgery has been successful beyond our wildest dreams. I cannot properly express in words the profoundest gratitude of our entire family, including nieces, uncles, and all in-laws. Suffice to say, you will reside in all of our prayers forever. Please wire via Western Union the final payment in the amount of Two Thousand One Hundred and Fifty Euros (€2150), to the account you already know, for it is perhaps not safe to include its number here. I need not remind you that, lacking the final payment, all my wife will be sold at auction before next month. With gratitude extending far downward and inward from a surface, sincerely and expectantly yours, Doctor Sade Reduviid, PhD, LLB, Esq. etc. It's important to verify this letter every time, the smart money sententiously reminds you, inspecting it for the least variation in diction and syntax. That's true, you say, studying the return address on the envelope. Apt. D, 1410 Montgomery Street, San Francisco, 94133, you muse. This is in North Beach, for chrissakes. The smart money narrows it down to Telegraph Hill, maybe even Coit Tower, north of Union Street. Corns calluses and bunions, you declare, it'll take us a week just to get over there. You reconsider the photograph. A handsome woman. Pretty, even, and what do you know about it, the smart money starts in. If there'd been any design changes in the last twenty years—. Can it. You make as if to frisbee the photograph over the lip of the cliff. Hold on, now, the smart money says. Don't let's do anything rash. Then don't let's be so liberal with the insults. Point taken. Grumpy today, chortling tomorrow, it's bipolar geography. It was a long way to go, just to be turned away. You'd think we would know a bar in every district of San Francisco, that wouldn't mind serving the like of us a drink. Time was in this town, the smart money declares, you couldn't get away from them. Don't spit your bridge. Sententious, too, you add, today. Sententious and grumpy, abounding in pompous and ill-tempered apostrophizing. Market Street was one long bar, in any one of which a half-pint draft beer and a shot of rye would cost you all of fifty cents. A half-pint of piss, just the right color, and a brimming jigger of Flindered Gallinule, is more like it, you correct, three-two beer and enough esters to guarantee the shakes and atrial fibrillation fit to cavitate the feathers in your down vest. Them days, the smart money reminiscences, sleeping bags was the flannel type, green canvas on the outside, blue flannel on the inside, with little ponies imprinted. My upper-case G God, you say to the after-noon expanse of the Pacific Ocean, never this blue. True, agrees the smart money, but that about the bars is correct. These days, one is hard put to broach the threshold of an establishment will-ing to countenance the idea that a man down on his luck might still want a drink, let alone, serve one to him. I believe that the entire substance of your solipsism, you and the smart money say in unison, can be boiled down to precise ratios of carbon, hydrogen, and oxygen. If you're trying to say ethanol and find-ing your tongue tied, that would be correct, C_2H_5OH, the very thought fires the will and we're on the move again, it would seem. Tireless apostasy, the smart money agrees. All else is pre-tension. If the odoriferous plume of molecules left by our pas-

sage were only visible, our tireless apostasy would be self-evi-
dent. Cannot we manage a drink, before the reconnoiter? Is it
not a precept of your method, the smart money reiterates testily, that all work be conducted in all sobriety, maximizing there-
by the chance of fruition, while minimizing that of doing one-
self injury? If we're being followed, they must be exhausted,
you suggest. They seem to like to talk in bars. That's true, but
everybody does. So what if we made a fake? How's that. We,
you know, duck into a bar, order a Shirley Temple, and see what
happens. Doesn't a Shirley Temple cost just as much as a martini? If I ran a bar, it would indeed. So what's the point? Non-
obfuscation, is the point. Clean, sober, ready to perform. Let's
duck down 47th Avenue, diagonalate Golden Gate Park via
John F. Kennedy to Martin Luther King, Jr., and duck over to
Irving on 41st, where there just about has to be a bar that will
accommodate us. Good idea. But—how much money do we
have? As you walk down the hill you pull out a fistful of filthy
ones from the ones stash and fives from the fives stash and a
single ten from the tens stash. Plus there's some change. Use it
for parking. Ah ha. Ah ha? Ahhhh ha ha ha....No metric can
compass this illness called Life. Thirty-two dollars. It'll have to
do. But to think about wasting it on a Shirley Temple....Well,
maybe just one. You think? I just hate to think of you as unable
to have a drink when you want one. It's just that *moderation*
seems to be a term unknown to you, beyond your understand-
ing. Like imagination? No, imagination is locked out. Try not to
think about it. Pretend you lost your password. Besides, why
imagine horror when you're surrounded by it? Surely, there are
other things to imagine? How about a life of sobriety? My lower-case g god, how can you even suggest such a thing? Well,
don't imagine, just think about it. First of all, your intestines
wouldn't be making those noises all the time. And your liver

wouldn't precede you everywhere you go. You could remember
what happened to you last night, with whom you exchanged
words, and about what. Many if not most of your matutinal con-
tusions might perhaps be eliminated. It's conceivable, anyway.
You might be able to keep some proper meat on your bones,
the rubicundity of your upper torso might subside somewhat,
edema, that swollen aspect of your extremities, notably in your
hands and feet, wrists and ankles, might subside, along with the
voices in your head and the tinnitus in your ears, along with
your blood pressure, along with your lipids, and almost immediately you would find yourself in funds sufficient to eat hot
meals any time of the day, and to sleep in a bed with a roof over
it and your own key to the door. Sounds like fucking heaven,
you say, stuffing the ones back into the ones pocket, the fives
into the fives pocket, the ten ditto, and keeping the change to
rattle ruminatively in the palm of one or another of your shaking hands as you walk. Set change to autojingle. Your walk is a
rolling sine wave, not dissimilar to a multiply-inflected limp
peculiar to that of an amphiuma whose semi-vestigial tootsies
have long since been gnawed to gists by itinerant athletic
coaches, but to memory dim of purpose, like the email address
of the second President Bush, which now attracts nothing but
spam. But it is an ambulation of surprising vigor, fueled as it is
by hatred, pain, and spite, as well the fervor of the turncoat. For
in fact, there is no thirst but the thirst, and no will but the will,
and no purpose but the purpose, and these shall maintain, uninterrupted, until they are extinguished. In due course, having
assiduously ignored the various salients of one of the finest
parks in the world, there, when you come to a certain, as if pre-
destined door, you stop in front of it and say to yourself, I never
noticed this place before. A grill over the door is open to the
sidewalk, the door itself stands in partial shadow, opening onto

an inviting gloom. A certain effluvium, equal to your own but enticingly fresh, cool but also rank, breathes from the doorway, a fetor seduced thence by the warmth of the sun, the calories of the former as if drained into the entropy of the greater exterior. To the right of the door is the frame of a window, waste high to slightly overhead, into which has been inserted a piece of plywood, and onto which is painted, in script, *Maxilla Salute*. This must be the place, the smart money announces. Who would have thought. Indeed it's a bar, and there's a woman behind it. She's older than you are—a good sign. Better, when you take a seat as far back in the gloom as you can get, to still face the door while seated at the bar, she folds up her *Chronicle*, lays a cocktail napkin on the bar in front of you, and waits. Best, when you order a Shirley Temple, she bursts out laughing and makes not one move toward glasses and bottles. Rather, she continues to wait. What's a maxilla? you ask. The drink or the anatomy, she replies without hesitation. Let's start with the drink. First things first, she concludes. That might be the case, you reply. Depends on how stupid it is. She smiles. Two ounces tequila, one ounce of pale ale, the juice of a fresh lime, two ounces of sweet and sour, salt to taste. Jesus uppercase H Christ, you expostulate, I pass. The moment you walked in the door, she says, I took you for a sensible person. Let's have a vodka martini, you say, ice cold, vodka from the well, two of the small olives, if you have them, and just the slightest hint of dry vermouth. That'll be my pleasure, she says. She retrieves a bowl full of mixed nuts, little cheese-flavored crackers, pumpkin seeds, two different colors of raisins, and places it on the bar. The protestations of the smart money are as if suffocated by a cushion borrowed from dead center in the eighth row of the oldest burlesque house in Buffalo. And the anatomy? you ask. Mammal or insect, she replies, as she breaks out the bottom half of a cocktail shaker and drags it through a sinkful of ice. You answer question with question, the smart money points out, abruptly alert to the moment. Unnecessarily, you point out. My dead husband was a DUI lawyer, she explains. Plus, he named the bar. Oh. If it's a human, she continues as she builds the martini, it's one or another of the two bones that form the upper jaw. My ex's idea was, if you're amused enough, the maxilla lifts, along with your head, like this, Ahhhh ha ha ha—see? You see a perfect upper plate of artificial teeth. You throw your head back in absolutely sincere laughter. Oh, you say, somewhat dully. Can I ask you a question? Sure. What's so goddamn funny? Everything, the bartender says, or nothing. Now we're talking, the smart money says. No in-between you say. That's the case, open and shut, my ex always said. Himself, he preferred to look at the bright side. In fact, he got paid to look at the bright side. He had guys, and gals too, with three, five, even six DUIs. They were always in here laughing it up. I thought you went to jail after three, your say. Depends on your lawyer, she replies. Obviously. Like everything else. But it was the old days, too. The whole courtroom would be full of drunks. Your honor, the DA would say, so-and-so here before the court blew point oh eight on the Breathalizer. Ah, big deal, the crowd would mutter, barely qualifies. Time was, legally drunk was point one two. One and a half times as much. That's true, you nostalgicate. Order in my court, the judge would say. And it was always the same judge in those days, she added. Driving Under the Influence was his bailiwick, you might say. She lands a martini on the napkin in front of you. It's so cold and so full you can't pick it up. The conical glass is a large one, two. It holds, as you happen to know, four fluid ounces. That'll be eight dollars, she says. Eight dollars, you begin to remonstrate. But anywhere else, that thing in front of you is two martinis, the smart money points out, and therefore sixteen dollars. I know, you smile, I was just taking the piss. You want I should start a tab? the bartender asks sweetly. Oh, man, you growl, after sucking the top three molecular layers off the surface tension. The vodka is so cold, and your haste is so perfect, you don't even feel the toothpick prick your upper lip. Where have you been my whole life? Right fucking here, I daresay is the answer. She pencils a hash mark on a note pad next to the cash register. So after they fine the first guy and turn him lose with a mild admonition, they lead in the next guy from the drunk tank. Now, your honor, the DA says, so-and-so here blew point one two blood/alcohol ratio on the Breathalyzer. And the crowd waiting along the back wall makes appreciative noises. Order in my court, the judge says, and raps his gavel. You gainfully employed? he asks the offender, and if the guy says yes, he fines him a hundred dollars and let's him go with a stiff admonition. If the guy says no, he doesn't fine him and he doesn't admonish him either, he just says that'll be ten days on the farm, where you can get thirty square meals and a hard week's work in the hot sun. Next case. Now, your honor, says the DA, reading from his stack of papers, so-and-so here blew point six two blood-alcohol ratio on the Breathalyzer, and the state thinks that's really too much, it's over twice the legal limit. And the back of the gallery breaks into applause and huzzahs for the guy. He's their hero. Not only that, your honor, the DA adds, squinting at a piece of paper, this is the third time Mr. So-and-so has appeared before this court. More applause and huzzahs from the railbirds. Your honor, my husband would jump in, because, frankly, if you're on your third DUI and you don't hire my husband, you're going to jail and without a drink for a lot longer than most people can stand, my client here is under a lot of pressure. I'll have another, you say, abruptly pushing the empty martini glass a couple of inches across the bar. She doesn't miss her stride at all. The shaker is in her hand and the hand is dragging it through the ice, and standing it on the rubber mat in the gutter admixes the sacrament before she has advanced another paragraph into her story. Plus his wife left him so he lost his house, and his job went south, too. You honor, and then my husband would turn to the gallery, who wouldn't want a drink? And the place would go nuts. Well, the judge might say. Mr. So-and-so, what resources do you have to fall back on? Now she's shaking the cocktail. In other words how is it that, despite these unfortunate circumstances as detailed by council here, how is it that you can afford to drink at all? Now that's a good question, your honor, my husband would invariably interrupt. She's pouring. But my client so-and-so here, he's got the Social Security, and he's got the unemployment. Is that a fact, the judge would reply. And he's got no place to live? She lands an icy, brimful martini on a fresh napkin in front of you, and rattles shards of ice out the little holes in the cap of the shaker. Which my husband lower-case g god rest his soul, used to call the Death Rattle Float. He's almost indigent? Yessir. And a wave of pity would ripple through the gallery. He's sleeping in his truck. And so, council, the judge would say thoughtfully, are you and the missus still renting out rooms? We are, your honor, my husband would reply. Are you willing to help Mr. So-and-so, here? And is he willing to be helped? And my husband and this poor sonofabitch so-and-so would exchange glances and they'd both shrug and my husband would turn to the judge. It would appear to be the case, your honor. And your head is now propped on the palm of one hand and the second martini is already half gone. Say, listen, the smart money begins. But you're listening to the bartender. Long story short, she's saying, there would be the hundred dollar fine, the license would be suspended for anything but a legitimate job, to which you can drive from home and back, but for thirty days only, AA meetings once a week for one month, and So-and-so would be remanded into the custody of my husband. The martini is two-thirds gone. How much money did we have? Thirty-two dollars, the smart money reminds you. I'll have another, you say, downing the last third of the second martini. And my husband would bring So-and-so home, the bartender says, tossing the diluted contents of the cocktail shaker into the dish sink and dragging it afresh through the ice. And we'd put the guy into one of the rooms upstairs and keep him down here all day for a month. Any checks that came in, he'd sign them over to the bar. In exchange he'd get his drinks, a place to sleep, and a hot meal every morning, if he wasn't in such bad shape he couldn't eat and a free ride to and from the AA meeting. She shakes the new martini with surprising vigor. Thirty days go by, he's either able to walk out of here and start his life over again, or he's not. If not, she decants the third martini, sooner or later, he'd drink himself to death right upstairs, there. She replaces the four-inch square napkin with a fresh one and carefully sets the third martini onto it, and applies the Death Rattle Float. And every year, that judge would get a nice ham for Christmas. You want those olives? she asks. You've been stockpiling them on a second napkin. You shake your head, no, as you apply your lips to the upper thirteen or fourteen molecular layers of fluid atop the martini. It's cold. The upper eighth of an inch of your tongue meat is now permafrost. It's good. Somewhere distant and far down in what passes for your soul the smart money is nagging. Don't sign anything, the smart money is saying. Pay up and get out of here. If it's an insect we're talking about, you say, how does the maxilla fit in?

THIRTEEN

PINK AND DISGUSTING MIGHT BEST DESCRIBE MY NEW DEMEANOR, bourgeois and pathetic might best describe my new arrangement with my new landlady, Mrs. Dunkeljaeger: all cleaned up, in fresh clothes with haircut, shave, and twenty bucks in my lint-free pocket right next to my louse-free *cuisse*, Social Security check signed over to her bank account, and a tab at her bar, which includes an evening meal, be I inclined to feed. It took three days, and you better believe I squawked. The Social Security website is bookmarked on her computer, as is a service that can produce a birth certificate in 24 hours. Curiously, about the second day in, my first person singular and plural pronouns and their possessives boiled down to the nominative I. The effect reminded one of some of the drugs they used to give one, about thirty years ago, back when certain institutions were making certain efforts on behalf of a certain definition of sanity. A Certain Sanity. It sounds, as they say in the newspapers, and in a lot of books, too, like a movie. It's yet another example of the a great paucity of similes in this country. A veritable avalanche of paucities, if you ask me, is what's wrong with newspapers, books, this country, and all movies; but never fear, Kulture, for hardly anybody ever asks me. Which is where I come in, observes the smart money. I thought you took the week off, you say to yourself. The smart money shakes what passes for his head. Back in the saddle. Now, opening the DayMinder, to catch up, you've now got four days to affect the job, or the contract expires, and even if you pull it off anyway, you won't get paid. Think of it this way, you recite in unison, if you don't get hold of that five thousand dollars, Mrs. Dunkeljaeger will be holding all your cards, only to dispense them to you at the rate of twenty dollars per week. That's barely bus fare, you balk. The time for balking, the smart money points out, is long past. Not to mention, you continue balking, at four times twenty equals eighty, that's about six hundred dollars a month less than my check. The time for doing that simple arithmetic, the smart money points out, could have been any of the elastic duration between birth and the third martini, first sipped at a certain bar—*Maxilla Salute*, you recall with a jerk of the chassis—, and long before you signed it all over. A place to live, you recall nostalgically. Crisp sheets, a creaking radiator, indoor plumbing, none of your crepitation of plastic bags ensnared by carousel wire. Curtains lifted by an on-shore breeze. Outdoor living, however, can be salubrious. Mostly. But regular cocktails, every night at five...On the chit...Which amounts to...? Well, the smart money counts on what passes for fingers, three nights running, you had the price of the first three martinis, since which there have been several others, last time you were conscious enough to add it up, carry the two, I think you're into Mrs. Dunkeljaeger for about a C-note. *What?* Plus tip. My god, you say aloud, I'm overextended. I hear you brother, says a man standing next to you at the stoplight. You hadn't noticed him before. Now you look at him. I beg your pardon? The man shakes his head. Far as I can tell, he says sadly, watching the red hand at the other end of the crosswalk, if I go to work at the Martinizing Depot six days a week for something like thirty years, and limit my cocktail consumption to whatever's available at weddings and funerals, I'll die with everything paid off. That's fantastic, you hear yourself saying. Ain't it the truth, the man says, stepping off the curb. Don't wanna be late, he adds, as if to himself, his stride lengthens, and he has accelerated halfway down the block before you've gained the opposite curb. What is a Martinizing Depot, you wonder aloud, and a man going the other way spins midstride and explains something about dry cleaning and patent applied for and trademark and copyright infringement before he turns full circle and almost immediately gains the curb from which you have just come. The signal changes and three lanes of traffic in each of two directions intervene between you and the intervention. Four days to get to Telegraph Hill, figure out the scene, and make your move, the smart money prompts you. Too bad we're never going back to that bar, you allow, as you progress eastward along Lincoln Way. You're cleaned up enough to take the bus, the smart money points out. What, you riposte, and drill down into my twenty bucks? At 9th Avenue you turn north, into Golden Gate Park. You got five grand coming, the smart money protests. Live a little. Job's not done yet, you reply stubbornly. You've never blown it before, comes the rejoinder. You is a professional. Yes. And like all professionals, it's the only thing you can do right. As for the rest—television, marriage, movies, family, filial piety, religious observances, advanced toilet training, talking in tongues, keeping up with your insurance, conscientiously answering your email, hygiene, blood in the stool.... They say professionalism will kill you but they won't say when, you reflect grimly. Talk about accruing retirement in the dark, the smart money comments with contempt. And you carry on like that as you diagonalate across the park. Grass, the smart money is waking up to the environment, sunshine, children. Lookit that dog catch that frisbee midair. Good boy. The scrubbing has not affected the period of your ambulatory sine wave, no more than it has cleansed your inner self of its inner self. Preposterous metabolics, you mutter. Meta Bollocks, the smart money counters, so many puns, so much money. A pleasant fantasy, you remark as you cross the horseshoe pit and exit the park at the corner of Stanyan and Fulton. Jog over to Anza, you suggest to yourself, it turns into O'Farrell. That's true, you answer, not without noticing the foul perspiration of a metabolism desperate to rid itself of the synthesis of alcohol. Sudoriferous, the smart money comments. Perhaps by the time you've attained North Beach you will have rid yourself of many of the salients of your new landlady's recent ministrations. One can hope, you react dully. All she wants is for you to die, the smart money points out. Is it really true, you change the subject dully, that once the liver runs out of the enzyme pertinent to the reduction of acetaldehyde to acetic acid, in desperation it infuses the surplus into the blood? You're changing the subject, the smart money comments, sort of. Is that why this perspiration reeks of acetylene and vinegar? Not only that, the smart money reminds you, it's why you get damn little nutrition when you're on a bender. I'm hungry, you're suddenly reminded. Plus, all those aspirin you take will eat your stomach lining. Maybe that's where the blood comes from. No, well, maybe, the smart money ruminates, but my money remains with the desperation of the body. If the blood too is toxic, then the body will try to eliminate as much of the toxicity as it safely can. And we know what elimination is. *Shise*, you whisper, will these voices never leave me alone? Take California, the smart money suggests. It's a real nice street. And if you head the other way there's Burmese restaurants. But if you carry on the way we're supposed to be going, there's streetcars. Another contraction through sheer usage, the smart money supposes. When is smart money going to become smartmoney? Or even Smartmoney? If it comes to that, you should make it Smart Money, thence SmartMoney. Get some cards printed up. You only got twenty dollars. No streetcars. Was a time, probably, it was hyphenated. Distant past. Back when people buried their cats sitting upright. When was that? So is that why I smell like leaking bottles in a welding shop? Acetylene and vinegar. Quite unlike crimson and clover. Dehydration and deli sandwiches. Huh? There's an excellent deli in North Beach. That Italian one, on Columbus Avenue. She almost threw away the envelope. That was heads up, telling her it was your daughter, and that you'd pulled the envelope from a dumpster in order to protect the photograph, that you'd not had any contact with her in a decade. Brilliant for two reasons, (a), it humanizes you, to a certain extent anyway, and (b) the thought that there might be a blood relation out there somewhere will force her to exercise a little caution as regards your natural death. Mrs. Dunkeljaeger, you pronounce, is one predatory chthonic harridan. With the stiff-bristle brush between the cheeks of the ass, she's quite vicious, replies the smart money, by way of agreement. You pluck at the inseam of your trousers. Good thing you're not going back. Ever. Take a left on Montgomery. Man, you cavil, that's one of the most uphill streets in town. So take a cab. Plus, it's discontinuous. No, no, that's Kearny. What about that generous tab? you wonder aloud. But now you're downtown where everybody assumes that, rather than talking to yourself, you're on the phone. You're never alone in a schizophrenic society, you marvel, looking around. It's true, you're fitting right in, the smart money encourages. When the westerly's up, you comment, nobody can smell that you're off-gassing. Mop your brow. Once was ironed, once did bloom, that kerchief out of your pocket. Now, it's rather drenched. You remove the envelope

from your pocket. Reading fourteen-ten Montgomery refresh-
es your memory. You should go by City Lights for a *Times*, the
smart money counsels, Give you something innocuous to do
with your hands while you're waiting. Masturbation is so un-
seemly. Divert up Kearny, cross Columbus at a corner bar
called Mr. Bing's, proceed up past Brandy Ho's Hunan Cuisine
to Jack Kerouac Alley, formerly Adler Place, and duck into City
Lights. Better read it while it still exists says a guy behind the
counter, looking up from his own copy, and, Sales tax went to
9½% as he totals the resister. Sorry, he adds, placing thirty-six
cents on top of the paper. I changed my mind, you say. Give me
my two bucks back. The fuck you say, the guy at the register
says. I'm carrying a knife, you hiss. So am I, the clerk responds,
I just got here. All right, you break out a grin, let's cut a rug.
Don't piss me off, the clerk responds. That's usually my line,
you say, but to tell you the truth, I've only got twenty dollars to
get me through the next week, and I forgot myself over this stupid New York Times. You know, you shrug, read it while you
still can. Well, why didn't you say so? We'll sell it to somebody
else. The clerk opens the register and hands you two dollars.
Upper-case G, God is great, you say, accepting them. That's
what I used to think too, the guy behind the cash register says.
Now I'm pretty sure it's lower case. I'll check back when I can
afford another paper, you tell him. Have a good one, the clerk
suggests, by way of salutation, though he's already got his nose
back in his paper. You're across Columbus, across Broadway,
and halfway up Grant Avenue before you tell yourself, that guy
didn't recognize me. Why would he, the smart money asks. Did
you recognize him? No, no, you tell yourself, there was a time
they wouldn't let me in the store. There was a time they would-
n't let Gregory fucking Corso in the store, either, the smart
money glowers, why not you? I'm not a bard, you stipulate,

mustering your dignity. So you do have your pride, the smart money marvels. If you can only do one thing at all, be the best there is. That's what your daddy always used to say. Fuck him and the plesiosaur he paddled up to the beach on. But it's true. It didn't start out that way. Let's go up Green. You think? Grab that Chinese newspaper. That'll fool 'em. This pineapple shirt is soaked through. So don't court no open flame. Steeper and steeper. What's a girl gotta do, in order to afford to live in a neighborhood like this? Owe money to the wrong people. Well looky here and whaddaya know, the fourteen hundred block. Pretty good. I walk this town like a Nantucket widow. It's really true, the sun's out in North Beach when it's not out anywhere else in town. Is it true that you can sweat out the poison? If we're talking about you, you'd probably not make no progress until you'd sweated yourself into a crepitating husk, quivering in a humid breeze, adhered to the bark of a walnut tree and abandoned by a molting locust. That serious? Here we are. Fourteen ten. You keep walking. She's youngish, she lives in this neighborhood, she probably has a job. What time is it? No idea. There's a bench down on the corner. Let's have a seat and read the Chinese newspaper for a while. Catch a little sun. I've had about enough sun. There's bars all over the place around here. You only got the twenty dollars until next week. You're forgetting the five thousand. That's counting chickens before they cheep. Yes, but it's been a long time since we had that kind of dough. Three months. Really? You are incredulous that you can master the urge for such a period. Let alone, focus it, channel it, so successfully. Little did your daddy know, you'd become such a success. That's the second time that sonofabitch has come up today. Probably the enforced 72 hours of hygiene has made allowances for queer eruptions of thought. Mummy from a bog. Her, too. Her and him need to be left out of the conversation, and remain out of it. Especially now, now that we are working. Formerly, and no doubt latterly, when the mind is merely stew, anything goes. But not now. Now, when we are working. But what about love? Is it true love, when you're not merely breeding? Is it true cancer, when you're not merely metastasizing? Even a railing, to put the feet up. Quite a view. This cleanliness, it's…Disconcerting? That's it. Just don't confuse it with thirst. Twenty bucks. That' not even enough for a cab ride back to the bar, where we could drink all night. I thought we were done with that place. Where's the harm? So long as Mrs. Dunkeljaeger thinks you have the daughter, she'll just let you drink yourself to death, which you intend to do anyway. Otherwise, no doubt, she has ways to accelerate the process. A quiver of methods, no doubt. The mattress smelt as one that has been died upon before, it's true. You'd think that, for the money at stake, she'd spring for a new mattress. So many puns, so much money. That'll be the day. You think, for the amount of booze involved, you would not have noticed a thing. True, but I'm sensitive. I never doubted it. What time is it? What time could it be? Looking at this Chinese, I feel ridiculous. If you could read it, you'd probably feel more ridiculous. Must be at least five. Let's take a turn around the block. Sure, just so long as it doesn't involve a bar. Understood. North on Montgomery to Union, west on Union to Kearny, south on Kearny to Green, north up the steps to the bench again. Salubrious, you wheeze to yourself, but you usually like to strike out for the long haul, from here to the beach and back, for example, especially when you are not in funds and about to go mad. Energetic, sinusoidal, vectored perambulation, mannered, as it were, and sudoriferous. These hikes mark the time between checks, between strikes, between paydays, between delousifications. Perhaps even a bath in the Pacific, to let the brine sooth the sores, cold as that might be. You recall a guy you used to see at Crissy Field. A long, long time ago, long before the restoration of the wetlands, long before windsurfing, let along kite-sailing, long before the goddamn motherfucking Disney Museum. Approximately halfway between the St. Francis Yacht Club, east along the beach, and the old Coast Guard Pier, to the west along the beach, there stands to this day a grove of Monterey cypress. Most afternoons, out of this grove, a naked man would appear, trot down to the water's edge, and plunge in. You had no idea who this man was. You didn't care. Each time you saw him you said, to yourself, a shroud without pockets. But you admired the fact that he expended not a thought upon the idea that anybody might find his nakedness offensive, let alone illegal. So you nodded hello to each other, over the years. And then, one day, you sinusoidaled down the beach as he was coming out of the water. This is it, he abruptly says. What is it? you say, surprised enough to respond. It's the first and only time the two of you exchange a word. Moving to Oregon, came the response. Really? Why? I've been seeing you here for years. San Francisco is over, man, the guy says, and he shakes his head. Way over. All around you were sunshine, the bay, the lascivious lapping of waves, the bluster of the afternoon westerly, cormorants, grebes, seagulls, a chevron of pelicans, and the towering spectacle of the Golden Gate Bridge. Really? was all you could think to say. Closing his eyes and lifting his face toward the sun, with both hands he pushed the salt water through his hair toward the back of his head. Really, he said. Oregon, huh? Oregon. Well, you said, good luck. He shook his head like a dog would, hair flying and droplets spangling. I'm making my own luck, he said, and he walked back up the beach toward the pile of his clothes in the cypress grove. When was that? the smart money asks. I think it was 1985. And, ever since, you've been feeling left behind. Don't piss me off. That's a long time to be left behind. Permanent and forever, one might say. Yeah, you agree, a generation. But Oregon? You got a —. What? There she is.

FOURTEEN

YOU SPIT OUT A TOOTH. THIS DOESN'T HAPPEN VERY OFTEN. YOU TRY TO get through the day without mentioning the teeth. It's a sore subject. So many puns, so much money, and why not? A man can dream. Consider: Remuneration for a thing so facile! She's home from work, one presumes. Not squinting against the light, like in the picture. Double-check the address, check. Her surname appended to buzzer lettered D, check. Now, how best to affect the hit? North Beach is a crowded, busy neighborhood. A lot of people know their neighbors, their names, their kids. She spoke to no one on the way up the street. Her arms were full of groceries, it's true. Normal-looking woman. About thirty-five. No wedding ring. Pretty, after a fashion, sturdy, too. Gym, perhaps. Athletic, maybe. Despite a desk job? Not your business, the desk job, not your business, her personality. But what could she have done to bring down the boom? Not your business, what brought down the boom. Your business the boom, not the *raison de boom*, but the boom only. And only two days, now, left to lower it. Another day, at a minimum, without a drink. The way of the warrior. Can't be helped. The piece is under a splice box adjacent the southern blast wall on the new, green Federal Building, which faces Mission Street, not far from the corner of Seventh. Retrieval mode, a good night's sleep and, some lower-cased d deity willing, task accomplished by nightfall tomorrow. Might get a leg up first thing in the morning, but nightfall for sure. Most people who have jobs start at nine. So maybe, if they live in North Beach and work downtown, they leave by eight o'clock, at the earliest. Time to lose the Chinese newspaper, at the very least. But hold on and, beseeching the sinusoidal, it's southward ho. Down the Montgomery steps, across Broadway to the Transamerica Pyramid. A little blood from where the tooth used to be. It made a soft click as it hit the sidewalk. Should have saved it? For what, eating lunch? A woman sat on the sidewalk, weeping. You've seen her before. She was weeping then. I want to go home, she was saying at the time. And so she continues to stipulate. Her musculature is still and recalcitrant, only the tears flow freely, a sign of powerful medication. You know about this medication, there was a time you were made to endure it as well. That time is past. You might render her advice on the matter, a shard of career guidance. But you are on a mission to Mission Street. And contract psychopathy isn't for everyone. At the corner of Merchant Alley and Montgomery you discern a trash receptacle, hard by the Chinese Educational Center. Perfect. You fold the photograph into the Chinese newspaper and tear them both to pieces. The pieces go into the trash can, and you spit. A thread of blood in the sputum. The envelope, you retain. Southward. The westerly persists. Plumes of dust and scraps of paper transect your path. Your philosophical existence has degraded, the smart money comments, into a single-minded pursuit. Every once in a while, you remind the smart money, one must step back from the adventure and endeavor to procure a living wage. Why is it, the smart money ponders aloud, that you cannot be content with your destitution, like everybody else out here on the street? It is not my way, you answer simply. The way of the martini, is the reply. Having closely shorn this setaceous husk of all wants and desire, you maintain, to the point of depilation, might one be forgiven, for turning a vice into a necessity? So long as you pay your way, comes the reply, almost anything can be forgiven. One mustn't entertain the thought of one's martini habit becoming a ward of the state. Upper-case G God forbid. The state can scarcely afford you as it is. As regards the martini, I ask nothing from the state. All I ask from the state is that they build overpasses that do not crumble at a mere wrathful glance from the odd deity, upper-case or not. To get the pistol now, or to get the pistol later? That is the question. It never hurts to be possessed of a firearm when sleeping in public. Besides, how long since you left the pistol under the telephone splice box on the south side of the Federal Building? Months. Since the Case of Riparian Sam. That would be three months. Do you think it's still there? How should I know? Best to check. If the piece is gone, we'll still have two days to do something about it before the contract expires. Jesus Christ, I didn't think of that. Should have gone straight there from Lafayette Park. But no, you had to bolt any number of celebratory martinis, and precipitate yourself into the clutches of a harridan into the bargain. How might she do you in, do you imagine? On the sly, you suppose, plutonium martini, like that. Not subtle at all, and much more expensive than your Social Security check could possibly be worth to her. Besides, she can't do you in until after you marry her. Marry her? She hasn't even proposed. Just you wait. And just how much trouble could that possibly be, after three or four of those large martinis with two or three of the very smallest olives? And—oh, I neglected to inform you of a germane observation: She stocks one quart, at least, of one hundred proof vodka. A quart, you say? A quart is plenty enough, to do a man in. Be that as it may, it's certainly enough to make him say I do. Or yes, at the very least. That's pretty thorough, not to mention insidious. I'll bet she has a justice of the peace as a regular customer. Why not marry him? He stops with two martinis, and is very particular about their not being more than eighty proof, and is well-known for leaving the second one unfinished on the bar. More for me, then. Not the point. One Social Security check comes to a Mrs. Dunkeljaeger, 3953 Irving Street, Apartment B, San Francisco, etc. But another check comes to a Mrs. Riley Bertram Abernathy, 3953-1/2 Irving etc., while yet a third arrives eager to be endorsed solely by a Mrs. Beatrice O'Riley, 3953 Irving St. Apartment 4, San Francisco etc. Get the picture? Where are all these guys buried? In Colma, for the most part, in close proximity to Wyatt Earp. Not to Calamity Jane? That would be a little too appropriate. No matter, we've already decided to forego a return visit to *Maxilla Salute*. She'll just wait. She knows about the appetite for the martini. Yes…When it comes to a choice between death or appetite, the latter wins every time. Besides, she's like the movie business. You mean—? That's right, she keeps any number of prospects orbiting their own corpse. West on Market. Oh no, please, skip on down to Mission. Market Street is too much like reality. You have a point. But Mission's not much further removed from reality. But there's the Cartoon Art Museum, and Yerba Buena Gardens, not to mention MOMA, and that incredible parking garage. Your taste in architectural and cultural salients wins me over. One wonders why they bothered to put the goddamn motherfucking Disney Museum all the way out in the Presidio. They try to spread the culture, all else being equal. Besides, the daughter paid through the nose for the privilege. Down here it's too expensive. Yes. You're playing with the big hotels. Yes. Entities able to shift vast populations of homeless people in favor of a minority of the rich. That's Communistic talk,

brother. At least it isn't Socialism. West on Mission to Seventh.
It's a wasteland. Them tall buildings abuilding will go a long way
toward fixing that. After a certain size, the lids on their dump-
sters are too heavy for one man to lift. Here we are at Fifth.
There went the Chronicle. I hear you on that. And now Sixth.
Approach with caution. The usual railbirds, taking in the sun. A
pair, to be exact, right in front of the splice box. They look
young. They know that guy in the green sleeveless sweater. He's
pretending to know them. They're guarded. It's all about cigarettes. Good. Can you make the wall? It's only twenty-four inches, for chrissakes. They're not even looking at you. Feel under
the stainless box, a plastic bag up against the far stanchion. And
there it is. Oh, says one of the boys. He's sitting on the low wall
with his back to you, but he's looking over his shoulder. Your
lunch? Already? It can't be lunch, says his friend, accepting a
light from the guy in the sleeveless sweater. Unless you're on
the night shift? He holds the cigarette so that it's cradled atop
forefinger, middle finger and thumb, and blows smoke up, into
the westerly. And you realize that this is a trio of homeless
homosexuals. They've both got sun-blazoned complexions, and
their skin is remarkably clear, too, but the roseate evanescence
of dissolution has already begun to suffuse the skin from below,
plus a touch of the puffiness symptomatic of edema. No, you
say to them, it's a gun. A gun, the first lad brightens, what you
going to do with a gun? It's a tool, you reply reasonably, stepping down from the wall. You stuff the black plastic package
into your belt. Think of it as a tool. I want it, the first boy says,
upping the wattage of what no doubt once passed for great sex
appeal. In the tenth grade, perhaps. In five years, or three, or
even two, while he will not have outgrown it, it will look pathetic. Today, he looks ready for anything, and, rather than effusing
a pang, as his partner one day would, his partner, who may per-

haps have been a little older, a little more experienced, a little more of a pimp, smiled, already stoned, long since up for anything. Naw, you say, backing away just a step before turning west. I gotta go to work. No no, the second boy says, you don't understand, he *wants* it, he really *wants* it. More nimbly than in years, and despite being now in the wrong direction, your sine undulates toward Eighth Street. The sun has set. The weight of the piece, though it weighs but little, is conspicuous in your waistband, though not as conspicuous as your pineapple shirt. This gives you a thought, and you continue down Mission Street, past Ninth and Tenth, until you attain the corner of South Van Ness, where stands the largest Goodwill outlet in San Francisco. Once inside, with a vector of purpose bordering on the monomaniacal, you purchase a fine example of a camel's hair coat, of the sort that can double as a blanket under all but the most extreme conditions. But it's the change of plumage that interests you more. The guy in the pineapple shirt who claimed to have scored a pistol under the splice box hard by the Federal Building may or may not have elicited some controversy amongst the rabble assembled there. By the hour, on the other hand, the hazard was excellent that everybody on that corner, as on most others, was already too far gone in their day to be retaining coherent gossip as regards a total stranger. Now to cases. Food? Food would wait for the morrow. Sixteen dollars remains of the twenty, camel's hair being perhaps unfashionable and therefore cheap. As to accommodations, Maxilla Salute remained out-of-bounds and far away besides, too far to walk after a day of, by the count of one's inner pedometer, between eight and nine miles of ambulation, as flies the sinusoid, which it doesn't, and, anyway, at the risk of being husbanded and harvested, a risk too mortal by half. The mind's eye casts about the neighborhood for a solution, some place safe to pass out from stress and exhaustion. Not far from the Opera, the Symphony, the Ballet—sopor assured. City Hall, too, to be dormant in the tendrils of bureaucracy. There's the Library as well, but too many homeless people already take advantage of the Library, it's grounds are a kind of sanctuary. The United Nations Plaza, where the nation of homeless unites. The Church of Scientology, hard by. Just around the corner, it's teeming with homelessness, crime, strife, despair, loneliness, and filth, not a cop in sight except on special occasions, like when the President's in town, where Seventh Street cross Market and, voilà, you're right back at the Federal Building, the greenest building on Uncle Sam's long list of properties. And so you go west, and then, after a while, west and a little north. You cross South Van Ness on Mission to Twelfth, one block and across Market to Franklin, north a couple of blocks to Hayes. And then you do the Hayes Street hill, one of the steepest in town, because you're crazy and enervation is good for your rage, you top the hill and persevere until you reach Stanyan Street, right next to St. Mary's Hospital, whose emergency room you know well enough—altogether, another four miles, as the sinusoid flew, which it didn't, for a day's total of some twelve or thirteen miles, as the sinusoid flies, which it hasn't. On the contrary. The pineapple shirt now smells like a rag soaked in xylene. Even the camel's hair coat has taken on a pungent tang. The coat's been way too hot, too, but you daren't abandon it, for the nocturnal fog of San Francisco would frost your bollocks without it, and its damp dilute your marrow. The lost tooth is forgotten, though the gap left behind, your fourth, in the lower rank, provides a succourous crèche for your tongue, one that you count, thus: Clockwise, tongue in the first, once; tongue in the second, twice; tongue in the third, thrice; tongue in the fourth, four times. Thence, counterclockwise: tongue in the third, five times; tongue in the second, six; tongue in the first, seven. And so forth. Alternatively, one might start in the fourth with one etc. And one will. One has. Somewhere between the back of McLaren Lodge, to the south, and the Horseshoe Pit, to the north, bound on the east by Stanyan Street and the west, more or less, by Conservatory Drive East, you crawl into the embrace afforded by the roots and lower limbs of a Monterey cypress, hard by its trunk. Somewhere out there stands a statue of Don Quixote, who at least had a friend, a horse, and a dream. You have neither the two nor the one. The fog soughs through the boughs of the cypress. And when you awaken in the morning, amid birdsong, the coat and your shoes are gone. It's a mockingbird. Perhaps it is in love. Its song is ineluctably enthusiastic.

FIFTEEN

BUT YOU BURIED THE PISTOL IN ITS PLASTIC SACK IN THE DIRT
among the roots of the tree, on top of which you slept. So the
means of production remain. But the lack of shoes is a threat to
your innocuousness. Down Hayes Street, five blocks east of
Stanyan, stands a cafe that's open very late. The sun is barely
up. In front of the cafe stands a pair of 96-gallon garbage trolleys, into one of which a man has thrust his upper torso to the
Waist. So many puns, so much remuneration. The lid is up on
the second trolley, and atop its load of refuse sits a styrofoam
plate containing a bagel, cream cheese, a few leaves of roughage,
and one and a half strips of bacon. You begin to eat this meal.
It's not bad. The bagel is perhaps no more than a day old. The
bacon is cold, not drained of fat, and tough. But it's also hicko-
ry smoked, a flavor you have not sampled for some years. The
roughage you leave. Head down into the first trolley, the man
continues to root about. In the window beside the door of the
cafe behind the two trolleys a slate proclaims the price of a
breakfast bagel at six dollars. As if it were a victory. Two pigeons
watch the scene from a respectful distance of six or eight feet.
The forager sounds like a rat making its way through a bed of
ivy. One of the pigeons darts along the sidewalk to the foot of
the trolley, beaks up a crumb of the bagel, and zigzags away as
if dodging gunfire. She is followed by her mate, and they take

turns pecking at their discovery in the middle of the street. Two blocks away, a garbage truck takes delivery of the contents of somebody else's trolleys. Willy-nilly, trolleys stand before every building on both sides of the street as far as the eye can see. The hand of the man emerges from the first trolley and sets another styrofoam carton atop the refuse in the second trolley, and returns to its work. You open the carton, revealing half an omelette, made with shallots with goat cheese perhaps, tomatillos on the side. A receipt lifts as if by magic and presents itself to you, scrawl up, and hesitates a moment before your eyes, while you read it, before it flutters sideways into the gutter, there to be momentarily inspected and dismissed by both pigeons. Not goat cheese but feta—what's the difference? Perhaps the ewe, suggests the smart money, as if just waking up, but, in either case, there's the brine preservative. It's like pulling teeth, you remark, while remembering to chew on just the one side, to get you to make any comment remotely germane. No puling teeth about it, ripostes the smart money, they pule when called, and top of the morning to you, too. The very sheath of misery, no two ways about it. A square meal, nonetheless and, but for a fork, perhaps the tetanus. For tetanus, one needs a deeper wound than the mouth. Is there such? In most cases, yes. Lame, you remark, apropos of nothing, is an anagram of male. A short silence. From the depths of the first trolley, rustling persists. In the street, the sire attempts to mount his missus while she's eating. Every situation will present its opportunity, remarks the smart money, no matter how opaque. Those shoes, for instance. I see they left you your socks. Everybody has their limit. They are perhaps the correct size. Nor are they out at the uppers. That would make it his turn. So far as that goes, he seems already fully engaged. Having fed you, he may well take pleasure in seeing you shod, too. You replace the styrofoam carton, now denuded excepting the tomatillos, atop the refuse within the second trolley, and drag the back of your hand over your mouth. He's been a deal of help, this fellow. We have left him his salad. Bent at the waist as he is, over the frontmost lip of the trolley, which is fully forty-two inches off the ground, he's tippy-toe, his shoes are easy targets. That bin makes for him a rather large phylactery, broods the smart money. Laceless, in fact, off they come. The figure stops rummaging. The socks are surprisingly clean. But he does not emerge from the cart. Perhaps he is contemplating the possibility of some fresh mortification. And behold, he has started to rummage again. What could possibly be in there, so deep? The man is merely thorough. And the odor? His milieu. His dedication to his task has saved him a thumping. To which you looked forward? Not at all, not at all. Not even a little? Not a whit. Nothing wasted, then. Empathy with the poor scavenger's degraded estate. None whatsoever. The truck is but a block away. He must soon emerge. Then we must away. A coffee would be good. Your stomach can no longer handle coffee. I'd forgotten. No matter. In three days, at the most, an hotel. And martinis. How much is left? Perhaps eleven dollars. They took your coat, they took your shoes, they didn't take your perineum. At Fulton and Ashbury, one descries a pair of sneakers, dangling by their laces from the south-facing stop sign. They are extremely large, though nearly new, but their laces take no time at all to remove from their former grommets and grommet them anew. Old grommet! delights the smart money. Frayed lace! No delight but in things, though you might have killed your fellow desolate. He is nothing to me, no more than I to anyone else. In failing to be hungover, you remain witless. I couldn't agree more. The view from atop Fulton Street is priceless—City Hall, the new, "green" Federal Building, the newly arrived edifice apparently at Fulton's eastern extremity, though much further away, on the very edge of the bay, its obscenity blocks the rising sun. And the moon, too, most nights; it blocks the rising moon. Will this vanity never be pulled down? Yours was pulled down years ago, and it's all you will ever understand of vanity, which, remaining buried and unremembered, amounts to a minusculity, untrafficked. Hammer flush every human salient. Defeat flocks like hoarfrost the slim blade of your being. Good morning, sirrah. Your customary sheath of misery? Perhaps there is time, this morning. Having fed, without bene-fit of coffee, lo these many years, and forward. Forward it is, deliberately ignoring the portent of this morning's lameness. Something isn't right. You've started off on the wrong foot, unshod, in a manner not usual. The sheath of misery fits uncomfortably, like it's shrunk in the dryer, another canker you can chalk up to immoderate cleanliness, plus or minus an evening passed out-of-doors, in the embrace of nature, as it were, nature red in toothlessness and traffic signal. Crimson, even. Got game? Not particularly. Yet persist one must. Please take into consideration the primal endurance of the mud that was and will be this flesh, and look out for that bus. Thank you. Why am I so tired? Good question. Maybe your enzymes is flagging. As go your martinis, however, you must persevere. Right you are, and perhaps there's still time. East on Fulton to Divisadero, right to Fillmore, left and all the way up Fillmore to Jackson. Not long after the turn onto Fillmore you pass a Goodwill outlet, but it's early, they're not open yet, and though they no doubt would provide a nice overcoat against the chill, perhaps later today, on the way back. That cypress off Stanyan isn't a bad place to wait out payday, a little more work in the bastionade department would make it reasonably secure, tin cans on strings, empty plastic bags on the ground, a scattergun, infrared perimeter intrusion detection—what else? A gallon of vodka, came the reply. Ah, back on task. Right on Jackson, run the ridge over Russian Hill and down through Chinatown, left on Stockton to Union, right and up the hill to Montgomery—et voilà…The sleepiest neighborhood you could want. The sun is fairly up, it is true. A flock of cherry-headed conures circle aloft, broadcasting their morning racket until the drove gets organized, then vectors off to one of their select hangouts, the Monterey pines in Washington Square Park, for example, or the palm trees down the early blocks of Dolores Street, or any of several especial groves in the Presidio or Golden Gate Park. You know them all because you visit them too. A jogger with a Labrador retriever on a leash chuffs up the hill. You assume your position on the bench. To the south stands the pyramid, the BofA building, the twin towers of the Hong Kong Hotel. Voices from up the street. A gate closes, and a young man wearing braces under his pinstripe jacket and carrying a briefcase makes his way down the hill, already on the phone, the heels of his shoes clacking. Three blasts on the horn of a cruise ship indicate that it's backing up, disembarking for Juneau or Honolulu or both. An electric car glides silently down the hill, takes a right on Green Street. Two children, almost certainly brother and sister, both wearing book satchels, walk hand in hand up the hill toward, no doubt, Garfield Elementary School, at the corner of Kearny and Filbert, just below Coit Tower. You wonder what time school starts. You wonder what time it is altogether. And then the gate over the entrance to fourteen-ten Montgomery Street creaks open, only to allow street access to another young fellow, dressed almost identically to the earlier one, a young man on the way to his office, gymnasium, cafe. The anecdotal evidence of these endeavors curls your lip. And as you turn around to refold your arms and scowl at the southerly view, still chilly in your long-sleeve pineapple shirt, the gate opens again, and she steps through it. She, too is dressed as if for a day at the office, though in slacks and practical flats. She could dress way up from this costume, you notice, she's an attractive young woman, and, once again, the fleeting query as to what she might have done to get you into her picture crosses your mind. But it's way too late for that now, for in reality she is the only thing between you and your next binge, and that's all she is. She comes down the hill, briefcase in one hand, phone in the other. She's taking the steps carefully, as it's steep. She passes you on the bench, and, favoring you with a polite smile as she grasps the handrail, begins the descent. You watch her. At the bottom of the staircase she turns right, onto Green. So if she's for downtown she's not for downtown yet, you conclude, she's going for her morning coffee. Seized by this intuition, you descend the steps yourself. At the bottom of the stairs you catch a glimpse of her at the far end of the block, taking a left on Green. So far, so good. You go straight on to Vallejo, where you descend a longer staircase, and on its next-to-last tread you take a seat. And soon enough, she appears on the corner and she takes a right, across Kearny, and heads west on Vallejo. You stand, thinking that, almost certainly, she's heading for the Cafe Trieste, which has held down that's street's intersection with Grant Avenue for two or three generations. Therefore you retake the stairs on faith, back up, and at the top you take a right and descend to Broadway. There, amid the sudden bluster of morning traffic, you take a right. A short block later you cross Kearny, and, soon enough, you take a right at the corner of Columbus. A very short stroll, north and up a slight grade, you turn the corner at Grant Avenue and, thirty yards later, presto, across the street is the Cafe Trieste, wherein, viewed from the street window, she waits in line. Outside the cafe on the Vallejo sidewalk there's a chair and a vacant table, page A-1 flapping atop a disheveled *Chronicle* beneath two empty cups, both still showing the remains of cappuccino foam. You co-opt table, chair, newspaper. "So You Just Want To Forget? Science Working on Eraser." "Korean Missile Was a Failure." "Pakistan's Ticking Clock." "Ranks of Homeless Swell as Middle Class Teeters." "No Easy Answer for Recharging Cell Batteries." You're just settling in for reading the newspaper, something you haven't done for a long time, so long you can't remember, and you're just beginning to wonder how long, it must have been the last time you were in Union Square, when a woman passes by. You wait, then look up. It's her. She's heading west on Vallejo. You go back to the paper. You shake your head. You deal the paper in to the table top in a heap, as if disgusted. She turns the corner, left, south on Columbus. You stand up, round the corner of the cafe entrance, and take your time walking back down Grant. Soon enough, she crosses the mouth of upper Grant at Columbus. She's carrying a covered paper cup in one hand, the briefcase in the other. No sign of the cellphone. You take a left at the corner. She's waiting for the light at Broadway. You read the menu in a window to your left. Pumpkin Papardelli, $9.95. Across Columbus, the red hand on the pedestrian signal begins to blink, and the numeric readout counts down from ten. When it reaches three, you begin walking. The hand stops blinking and remains on. The light turns red. The light in front of your quarry turns green. As she gains the curb on the south side of Broadway, you step off the curb on the north side. As you mount the southern curb, she's passing the mouth of Jack Kerouac Alley, formerly Adler Place. Across the street from her and down a little bit, at the corner of Columbus and Pacific, a big green neon cocktail glass lofts above Mr. Bings. MARTINI, the sign says, speaking to you, to you personally, and, with a growl of resolve, you quicken your pace. A helicopter passes overhead, low, seeking knowledge, perhaps, of traffic on the Central Freeway. She rounds the corner at the northern vertex of Kearny, where it cross Columbus, where she's caught the light, and she skips across Pacific there, just as the light turns green, and four lanes of traffic accelerate up Kearny, to split evenly at the X, two lanes north on Columbus, back up to Broadway, and two lanes north on Kearny, also up to Broadway. You have to wait for this traffic. But you can see her, as she waits as a car that has made a left across two lanes of northbound traffic, on Columbus, to enter a parking garage to her left. She removes the cover from the hotcup and has a sip of coffee. The car enters the garage. The light changes, enabling you to cross Kearny. You wait to cross Pacific. From here, you can no longer see your quarry. The pistol is tucked under your waistband at the small of your back, under the loose tail of your pineapple shirt, and you touch it. The Czechoslovakian cafe, you notice, has been boarded up. The light changes. Gaining the opposite curb, you walk through a glass door, into the elevator lobby of the yellow brick building on the south eastern corner of Pacific and Kearny, and back out the glass door at the far side of it. Down a wide flight of four steps and you are on the sidewalk of the Kearny, across the street from Columbus Tower, aka the San Francisco Flatiron Building. At the bottom of the block the light turns green, so she crosses Jackson. By the time you get there the light has turned red. You take a left on Jackson. There's no traffic so halfway down the block you jaywalk diagonally across the street. At the corner, you take a right onto Montgomery and see, at the bottom of the block, a woman waiting for the light at the three-way intersection of Kearny, Montgomery, and Washington. Across the street from her looms the open framework geodesic atop which stands the Transamerican Pyramid, whose footprint is half the block. The light goes green. Gaining the curb across Washington, she takes a left. The light goes red as you arrive. You turn east on the north side of the street. Halfway down the block stands a gate into a little pocket park that stretches along the east side of the pyramid, between Washington and Clay. North across Washington from this gate is the mouth of Hotaling Place, and connecting them is a pedestrian crosswalk, against whose right of way traffic must yield. You cross as she enters the park. At lunchtime today, any number of people will be scattered among the odd spot of sunshine reading, talking on the phone, eating. At the moment, however, there is no one. The park is deserted. You quicken your pace, pulling the gun. You rack the slide as you extend your arm. The pistol is a foot from the back of her neck when a blow strikes your shoulder and spins you around. Your pistol discharges harmlessly. Quite surprised, you see a man down on one knee in the middle of Washington Street, holding a pistol of his own with both hands, arms fully extended. His pistol is pointing at you. A man to his left faces the oncoming traffic with arms outspread. He's shouting. A tire squeals. The man with the gun looks at you, over his weapon, questioningly. You lower your pistol and, just as you fire at him, you receive another violent blow from behind. Your gun discharges, quite harmlessly. Again you spin, this time slowly. You notice a white cup rolling across the flagstones, streaming a brown liquid, from which steam arises. Her brief-case on the ground, mouth open, she is holding a pistol of her own. If it's a millimeter, it's nine of them, you are surprised to note. She looks surprised, too, and she might also have a ques-tion to ask. There is shouting. A wave of imbalance courses through your legs, it's like the '89 earthquake again, it's as if you're just off the deck of a ship after years before the mast. A shadow flicks over the park. You lower your pistol. She blinks, then begins to lower the barrel of her gun. A blow knocks you forward, your gun discharges, and its snap explodes a divot out of a flagstone in front of you. The smoking chips are barely disseminated before you bite the cavity with your one incisor, which is dislodged. Vertebrae crack. Your legs toss insensate aft of you, like scythed vines. You feel very little of this, but, for lack of a better term, it's as if you hear all of it. The younger cop is upon you, and you are disarmed. He wants to cuff you. To this end he locates one arm, but gore obfuscates the other. She is close. I didn't recognize him, the older cop is saying, though you can't see him. He cleaned himself up. That was fucking close, the younger cop says, angrily. She is staring at you, visibly upset. It's her first time, perhaps. It's okay, you telepath, it's the first time for both of us. Her distress is palpable. It's going to be contagious. Her pistol is in one hand. In the other, you can see, is her badge. She had wanted to show it to you. Now she's crying. Your heart, such as it is, goes out to her. Maybe this could be my daughter. Oh, says the smart money, now you're human. Where the hell have you been? Packing my bags. I'm out of here, I knew you'd go soft in the end, and the smart money goes up in smoke. Not on your life, you stipulate to the evanescing ghost, I'm maintaining my standards! Listen. Listen! Don't worry about this, this thing, you try to tell her, don't worry, you try to tell the smart money, don't worry, you try to tell everybody especially her, they're holding you down but you get it out with a roar, it's one less human being to despise.